HANNAH'S WARRIOR

COSMOS' GATEWAY BOOK 2

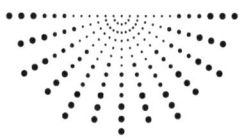

S.E. SMITH

ACKNOWLEDGMENTS

I would like to thank my husband Steve for believing in me and being proud enough of me to give me the courage to follow my dream. I would also like to give a special thank you to my sister and best friend, Linda, who not only encouraged me to write, but who also read the manuscript. Also to my other friends who believe in me: Julie, Jackie, Christel, Sally, Jolanda, Lisa, Laurelle, Debbie, and Narelle. The girls that keep me going!

And a special thanks to Paul Heitsch, David Brenin, Samantha Cook, Suzanne Elise Freeman, and PJ Ochlan—the awesome voices behind my audiobooks!
—S.E. Smith

Hannah's Warrior: Cosmos' Gateway Book 2
Copyright © 2012 by Susan E. Smith
First E-Book Publication August 2012
Cover Design by Melody Simmons
ALL RIGHTS RESERVED: This literary work may not be reproduced or transmitted in any form or by any means, including electronic or photographic reproduction, in whole or in part, without express written permission from the author.

All characters, places and events in this book are fictitious or have been used fictitiously, and are not to be construed as real. Any resemblance to actual persons living or dead, actual events, locale or organizations is strictly coincidental.

Summary: A gateway to another world has been invented, and thanks to a determined alien male who wants her, Hannah is about to go through, whether she wants to or not.

ISBN: 9781493701315 (kdp paperback)
ISBN: 978-1-942562-08-5 (eBook)

{1. Romance (love, explicit sexual content). 2. Science Fiction – Aliens, Portal. 3. Paranormal. 4. Action/Adventure.}

Published by Montana Publishing.
www.montanapublishinghouse.com

CONTENTS

Synopsis	vi
Chapter 1	1
Chapter 2	17
Chapter 3	26
Chapter 4	36
Chapter 5	45
Chapter 6	54
Chapter 7	65
Chapter 8	72
Chapter 9	81
Chapter 10	90
Chapter 11	99
Chapter 12	108
Chapter 13	116
Chapter 14	127
Chapter 15	139
Chapter 16	149
Chapter 17	159
Chapter 18	167
Chapter 19	174
Chapter 20	179
Additional Books	186
About the Author	191

SYNOPSIS

Borj and Hannah come from two different worlds…literally. On Earth, she built a life away from people – for good reason. On Baade, he spent a lifetime searching for her.

Hannah Bell, the oldest of the three Bell sisters, spends most of her time in the remotest parts of the world photographing endangered animals. She is also gifted with an extraordinary sixth sense that has saved her life more than once, and this time it's telling her something has happened to her littlest sister, Tink. When no one answers her calls, Hannah takes the first flight home, and discovers Tink's best friend Cosmos has opened a portal to another world! A world she is about to be taken to whether she wants to go or not.

Borj 'Tag Krell Manok has been assigned to bring a family member of his brother's bond mate to their world, and from the moment he sees Hannah's photo, he knows exactly who he will bring. He recognizes her immediately as his bond mate, and after so many years yearning for her, it is an incredible feeling to finally know who she is, what she looks like, and where to find her. The only problem is their first meeting doesn't exactly go according to plan! He's never met a woman so independent – and so effectively violent when she feels threatened – but it's a good thing Hannah is no stranger to survival, because Borj has no idea what his actions will lead to....

Internationally acclaimed S.E. Smith presents a new action-packed story full of adventure and romance. Brimming with her signature humor, vivid scenes, and beloved characters, this book is sure to be another fan favorite!

CHAPTER ONE

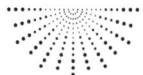

*H*annah Bell slowly focused the lens on her camera. It was the first time she felt like everything was just right. She had waited patiently for the past month to get a shot of this particular pride of lions. The male was a huge son-of-a-bitch and meaner than her sister Tansy when riled up.

And that, thought Hannah with a small smile, *was pretty damn mean.*

The lionesses were lying under the shade of a lone tree, absently keeping an eye on the cubs. The huge male was covered in scars from previous fights and was prowling around the females as if he could sense Hannah's presence. She hoped not. She was a good distance from the safety of her Land Rover and would never be able to reach it in time if he should decide to attack.

She had left her guide back in the vehicle, reassuring him she would be fine. By now, she would have thought he would get tired of asking her to come along. She always told him 'no'. He would just get in her way.

Hannah zoomed in taking several more photos. The lighting was perfect and she knew she was getting some award winning shots. She was about to take another series with a different lens when a shiver went down her spine. Hannah let the feeling come; keeping her eyes focused on the lions as she mentally sought what the shiver could mean. Tink... It was the first image that popped into her head and she knew something had happened to her littlest sister.

Hannah slid the lens cover over the lens of her cameras and slowly crawled backwards across the dry, arid ground. There was still another hour of good lighting to take more photos, but the Bell family had one rule they lived by... family came first, always. Hannah's instincts were always right.

Those instincts were what saved her life on more than one occasion during some of her more dangerous photo shoots. Once she felt she was far enough away from the lions to move faster, Hannah jumped to her feet and began jogging back to the Land Rover ignoring the sweat running down her back or the thump of the camera bag against her side. One thought kept running through her mind; something happened to Tink.

"You are back early," Abasi said in Swahili. "Were the lions not there?"

Hannah pulled her camera bag off her shoulder and carefully packed the two cameras around her neck in it. "They were there. I need to get back to camp. We need to get to the closest village. Something has happened to my baby sister," Hannah replied.

Abasi didn't say anything but quickly moved around to the driver's seat sliding in just as Hannah slid into the passenger side. He didn't question Hannah's knowledge that something was wrong. He had worked with Hannah for the past two years and knew if she said there was a problem, there was a problem. He believed Hannah was touched by the spirit held within the Earth itself.

The drive back to camp was long and dusty. There was a mild drought in the region, but Hannah could smell the rain in the air. Storms in Africa were as unpredictable as the wildlife. It could be calm one moment and violent the next. Hannah slid out of the Land Rover and jogged over to her tent.

She quickly packed the few odds and ends that were out while Abasi started breaking down the rest of the camp. She had very few possessions, mostly just her camera equipment which she took extreme caution with as it was her lifeblood. Her clothing was always packed and ready to move at a moment's notice.

Storms and wildlife were not the only thing unpredictable in the regions she went to. More than once, Hannah found herself in the middle of a government change. She had won a few awards and international recognition for her photographs of the effects of those changes on the people, land, and wildlife and two scars from bullets from disgruntled rebel leaders who did not like what she was showing the world.

Hannah pulled the strap of the canvas bag with her cameras over one shoulder while picking up her backpack with her clothing in the other. She glanced around to make sure she had everything before heading out to the Land Rover. She placed both in the back seat.

She turned and headed back to get the low, folding cot she used as a bed. She quickly folded it and placed it and the lantern in the very back. By the time she did that, Abasi was already breaking down her small canvas tent. She quickly helped him.

In less than half an hour, they were bumping over the rugged terrain heading for a distant village in the lower regions of the mountains. Hannah glanced at her watch. It would be late when she called Tink, but her little sister was just going to have to deal with it. Hannah wanted to know what was going on. The feeling something dire had happened was getting stronger causing Hannah's gut to twist in unease.

Hannah waited impatiently, pacing back and forth in the small village on the border with Tunisia. It was the closest village to where her last shoot was. Abasi was talking quietly with a small group of men. He had been against them coming so close to a country known for its instability and wanted to see if any of the local tribesmen had noticed anything recently.

Hannah growled in frustration when she heard RITA's voice come on the line. "Good afternoon. This is RITA. I'm sorry, but neither Tink nor Cosmos can come to the phone right now. May I take a message?"

"RITA, this is Hannah. I need to speak with Tink as soon as possible. Tell her to call me as soon as she gets this message. I don't care what time it is. I have the satellite phone on and am in a small village right now," Hannah said impatiently.

"Oh, Hannah… How are you doing, dear? Are the pictures of the lions turning out nicely?" RITA said in an exact replica of her mom.

Hannah gritted her teeth and bit back an expletive. *Why her sister would create an exact duplicate of their mother Hannah would never know. It wasn't like the world needed, or could even handle, another Tilly Bell in it,* Hannah thought as she fought to control her frustration. The feeling eating at her gut was beginning to piss her off.

"Everything is fine here, RITA," Hannah said, drawing in a deep breath to calm herself. "What is going on with Tink?" Hannah glanced over at Abasi as he followed her with his eyes. From the look in them, they might need to move to another village pretty soon. Hannah gave him a brief nod, watching as he turned and spoke quickly to another man.

"Oh, Tink has been on the most marvelous adventure. I know she will want to tell you all about it when she gets home. You aren't going to believe it! I'm so excited," RITA began before her voice faded. It was the fading part that caught Hannah's attention.

"But…" Hannah bit out waiting for RITA to finish.

"Well, there was one slight problem… but I think it might be resolved soon," RITA said with a slight upbeat note to her voice.

"Just tell her to call me ASAP," Hannah ground out before disconnecting the call.

Hannah let her head fall back in frustration and stared up at the slowly darkening sky. Something was wrong. She knew it. She could feel it all the way through to her bones. RITA was a combination of her baby sister, Tink, and her mom's new software programming. RITA stood for 'Really Intelligent Technical Assistant', a self-adapting voice recognition computer program that could learn and adapt to the changing environment. It was the beginning to an artificial intelligence program her mom was working on the last time Hannah had been home.

Hannah frowned at that thought. It was almost two years since she last saw her family. This was the longest she had ever gone without seeing one or more of them. Hannah jerked back to the present when she felt a slight weight on her shoulder. Looking over it, she saw Abasi watching her intently.

"We need to leave here as soon as possible. Soldiers have been spotted about ten miles out heading this way. The villagers are sending their younger women and small children into the mountains to hide. The last time the soldiers came five men were killed, several of the women were raped, and almost a half-dozen young boys taken. It is best if you are not seen," Abasi said quietly but firmly.

Hannah bit her lip and nodded. She knew all too well the dangers for women in any part of the world. A dark memory flashed through her mind before she pushed it away. She believed in all the teachings of her parents. They could spout mottos and words of wisdom like no one else she knew and they proved right every time. Nodding again, she followed Abasi to the Land Rover. She glanced around at the small group of women and children being escorted out of the village.

"Will they be alright, Abasi?" Hannah asked sadly. She hated this part of humanity. It was one reason she preferred to be on her own away from everyone.

"Yes," Abasi said as he turned the Land Rover around and headed out of the village. "They have learned to take precautions. I spoke with several of the elders of the village and the soldiers will find nothing in the village but old men and a few heads of undernourished cattle."

Abasi took them about twenty miles away, parking the Land Rover in a small gulch. He and Hannah quickly covered the outside of it with dried branches. Abasi explained the gulch was high enough that even with the rains to the north they should be safe enough for the night. They piled what they could in the back of the Land Rover and made a bed in the back seat. Hannah would take the first watch for the night and Abasi the second. They had done this numerous times over the past two years and had it down to a science.

Hannah pulled her jacket closer around her as she settled down on the top of the Land Rover. She felt it rock a little as Abasi settled down inside before all was quiet. Truth be told, Hannah loved this part of her life. She enjoyed the peace and quiet of the night and the beauty of the stars untouched by artificial lights or pollution. In the distance she could hear the sounds of the night predators as they moved. The sounds of the snorts from wildebeests and the faint roar of a lion filtered through the cool night air.

Hannah let her mind wander as she stared out into the darkened landscape. She wondered what type of 'marvelous adventure' her baby sister had gone on. Jasmine 'Tinker' Bell was the light in the Bell family. Her petite size and infectious personality lit up any room when she walked in. She was three years younger than Hannah, who was twenty-five, although, Hannah often felt much older.

Their parents had the three girls within three years of each other. None of them were planned, but all of them were loved. Their dad, Angus, was a successful science-fiction writer while their mom was a bit of everything. Tilly Bell could work on any motor in the world if given a wrench and ten minutes and program a computer any hacker would have a problem getting into. She was just as hyper as Tink, while Hannah was more reflective like their father.

Tansy, Hannah thought for a moment with a soft smile, *well, Tansy was probably an invention of their mom's as she didn't really fit under any category Hannah had ever figured out.* Even as a kid, Tansy had always been different. She was the strong, quiet type that could see right through you or scare the shit out of you depending on the situation. It was almost like she came from one of their dad's science fiction stories. But, then again, Hannah couldn't say too much as she was different too, especially since Nicaragua.

A shudder went through Hannah as she let the memories come. She learned a long time ago to just let them flow through her so she could let them wash away the pain and guilt. She used to try to bury them, but found it just made it worse. Each time she let the memory come, it seemed to help make it a little less painful. *At least they weren't coming near as often,* Hannah thought with relief.

Her parents spent the better part of a year trying to get her to open up about what happened, but Hannah never told them everything, she couldn't. Hannah knew they felt extremely guilty about what happened, but Hannah never blamed them. In a way, it became a blessing. Her parents always said there was a silver lining to everything that happened in a person's life. In this case, Hannah learned to trust that feeling she gets when something is about to happen or when it tells her to do something. She would have been dead or worse dozens of times if she hadn't learned to accept it.

Hannah let her eyes move over the darkened landscape as she let the memories flow through her to when she was fifteen. Her parents were in Nicaragua for a meeting with an oil conglomerate to discuss some new power generator her mom was working on. Her mom had her degree in mechanical engineering with a specialty in power grids and generators... *probably a throwback to working in her grandfather's garage when she was growing up,* Hannah thought distractedly as she watched the shadows of a group of hyenas go by.

Hannah pulled the jacket closer and folded her arms around her knees. She knew as long as there were predators and the night sounds around them, they were alone. She refocused on the memories determined to let them run their course. She remembered how excited all three girls were to be at the big function the oil company executives were giving. There was a huge reception with dinner and dancing.

When you spent most of your life in a home with ten wheels and one closet-size bathroom, it was a dream come true to have a huge bedroom all to yourself. Hannah being the oldest was allowed to stay up an hour later than the other girls. There were several handsome young boys in attendance and Hannah was surprised at all the attention she was getting. Her parents made sure they never let her out of their sight, which truthfully, Hannah was perfectly happy with since she didn't know how to handle all the attention she was getting.

It was as she was having her last dance when the gunmen burst in. Hannah remembered staring in shock as the dark red splatters of blood covered her dress as the men opened fire on several of the guards. The boy dancing with her was hit by one of the bullets. Hannah watched in horror as the life faded out of his eyes and he collapsed in front of her. Several of the guards had grabbed her parents and the two top members of the oil company and their wives and thrust them into a 'safe room' sealing them inside while the gun battle raged outside in the ballroom.

Hannah remembered as if it was yesterday being knocked down by the people fighting to escape the bloodshed. She lay in the blood soaking the floor near the body of the young boy who moments before held her in his arms. When the gunfire stopped, the masked gunmen began jerking up those who were not hurt and pushed them out into several trucks. Hannah had been one of the ones grabbed.

She was numb with shock and unable to understand most of what was being said as her Spanish wasn't good enough to understand it when it was spoken so fast. She didn't remember a lot about the actual trip to the rebel camp deep in the jungles, but she remembered the crying, the fear, the dark, and the never ending twists and turns the trucks took to get there. It was dark again by the time they arrived.

The women were led into a small wooden hut while the men were placed in open cages. Hannah remembered looking around and realizing she was the youngest one there. There were two other girls a couple of years older and their mother and two other women she vaguely remembered being introduced to.

She spent three days living in terror as one by one the women were taken out. Hannah could hear the screams before the silence. As each one was brought back, the blankness in their eyes scared Hannah more than anything else. She could hear the laughter of the men as they brought them back and the anguished screams of the men in the cage as they were tortured.

Hannah knew when it came time for them to come to her, she would fight or die. She refused to become a hollow shell of a person. Her parents taught her how to fight, how to defend herself and she would. It was funny, but she could feel it was time for her to do something.

Hannah had spent the last two days working on loosening one of the wooden boards that was cracked. It broke off and one end made a sharp, jagged point. Using a piece of her dress, she tore some of the underskirt off and wrapped it around as a handle.

Hannah looked through the cracks in the wall at the jungle surrounding the small camp they were in. She had always felt at home in the wilderness. Perhaps it was because of all the places they had lived and her love for exploring the wilderness and photographing it. She didn't really know. Whatever the reason,

Hannah would rather take her chances with the jungle animals than with the human ones.

Hannah felt the sweat drip down her back as the next wave of memories washed over her. Two men came this time. They called for one of the girls who were close to Hannah's age and Hannah. The girl started crying softly as the man yelled at her again to get up and follow him. Hannah moved silently holding out her hand to the girl when the man took a threatening step towards her.

The mother of the girl got up and started forward begging the men to let her go in her daughter's place. One of the men, a short, heavyset man stepped forward, striking the woman across the face hard. Hannah looked on in horror as the woman flew back against the side of a small table and fell to the dirt floor, not moving. None of the other women, including her other daughter, moved to help her or see if she was alright.

Hannah could feel the rage building as the memories came. Her fists clenched into tight balls as if she was once again holding the broken piece of wood like a knife in the palm of her hand. Hannah's eyes flashed to a shadow in the sky as several bats flew over the gulch. She forced her hands to relax and drew in a deep breath.

Hannah closed her eyes briefly allowing the sounds of the night to calm her as the images flashed through her mind. She remembered the hatred that swelled through her like a tsunami rushing toward shore. She remembered the men laughing as they pushed both of the girls out of the hut.

Hannah walked with her head high, glancing about as she moved looking for an escape route as the girl next to her cried softly. Hannah let her gaze slide to the men in the cage. Most of them didn't move. There were a couple who followed Hannah and the other girl with their eyes, but they didn't say anything.

Hannah cringed as one of the men touched her hair and said something. Hannah recognized the crude words and shuddered as revulsion swept through her. In that moment, she was no longer an innocent young girl, but a woman determined to survive… even if it meant killing another human being to do it. She was about to become one of the predators of the jungle.

Hannah could feel something inside her break free and knew it was time to trust in the feelings coursing through her body. As soon as the men pushed her into the small hut Hannah moved. She swung the sharp point up into the throat of the man closest to her, piercing his jugular.

The only sound he made was a gurgling sound as he gripped his torn throat before he collapsed onto the dirt floor. The other man, intent on the young sobbing girl in front of him, never saw the sharp point that pierced his throat from the back. Hannah ignored the blood pouring down over her hands and arms as she pulled her makeshift knife from the man's throat. She remembered quickly, turning and shutting the thin wooden door of the hut so no one else could see what was going on inside.

Hannah glanced at the girl sitting on the ground rocking back and forth, no signs of awareness in her eyes. Hannah leaned down and tried whispering to the girl to get up and follow her... but the girl just curled up into a ball on the dirt floor whimpering. Hannah knew she had no choice but to leave her if she was to find help for the others or save herself. The girl would get them either captured or killed. Hannah whispered a soft apology as she ran her hand over her dirty hair, but she doubted the girl even heard her.

Hannah moved to a low window in the hut saying a word of thanks that the back bordered the dense jungle. Within moments, she had disappeared into the thick foliage. Hannah remembered the fear of being alone and lost for the first couple of nights before she began realizing, being in the jungle was less frightening than being held captive by the rebels.

It took her ten days before she came to a small village along the Rio Coco. By then, she looked more like a wild woman than the elegant young girl who two weeks before had attended a dance. Her hair was a tangled braid down her back and her dress was in pieces. She had used strips of it to bind around her shins for protection and had blended in dirt to hide the color of it as much as possible.

The first two days she spent a good deal of her time hiding either in the trees or under the thick ferns and other undergrowth as the rebels searched for her. By the third day, they seemed to feel she was probably dead. She survived by drinking rainwater from the leaves of plants and eating what few pieces of fruit she could find. To help protect her from the bugs, especially the mosquitoes, she applied thick coatings of mud to her skin.

With a quiet resolve to survive so she could help the others, she began moving west towards the glimpse of the river she was able to see from the top of one of the trees. She slept in the trees at night, tying herself to them with vines to keep from falling out. During the ten days it took to find her way back to civilization, Hannah realized one thing... she would never be the same.

Hannah gazed up at the stars and let out a series of deep breaths as she felt the same resolve that gave her the strength to survive the jungles flow through her now. She understood the world... the circle of life. In order to live, she had to kill. She would always regret the need to take a life, in her case, two lives, but she understood the necessity of it. She saw it in every species she photographed. From the lions to the ants, there were always a predator and a prey. It was up to her to decide which she was going to be.

She smiled as she watched a meteorite flash across the starlit sky. Hannah chuckled softly as she made a ridiculous wish. It would seem even she still had childish dreams. Hannah's eyes jerked down as she heard the distant sound of an engine. Sounds could be deceptive out in the open like this. The vehicle could be twenty miles away or two. Hannah listened carefully, but it soon faded. It was crazy to be driving at night under any conditions in this region. Lights could be seen for miles and the roads were treacherous enough during the daylight. Hannah suspected it must be some of the rebel forces from across the border, more than likely smuggling guns or drugs. Either way, she was glad they were well hidden.

As she settled back down, she let her mind finish taking her down memory lane. Hannah grimaced at that description of a very bad time in her life. *Well, it wasn't too bad.* Hannah had to admit. *She did meet Jacq and Maria.* Hannah had tumbled out of the jungle near the cantina they owned on the river. Maria was throwing out some dirty wash water when she spied Hannah standing just outside the thick growth of the jungle. She had taken one look at Hannah and let loose a long line of Spanish curses.

Hannah would have been afraid if it hadn't been for the look in her eyes and the feeling telling her the curses weren't directed at her. The next thing Hannah knew she was being guided into a small room in the back while Maria yelled for Jacq. Hannah mumbled out her story about the other captives while Maria carefully washed and cleaned the numerous small cuts on Hannah. Jacq used a satellite phone to contact the local authorities with the information Hannah was able to give them.

The next week was a bit blurred. Hannah remembered Jacq taking her up river to a larger town where her parents tearfully met her along with Tink and Tansy. Hannah later learned most of the hostages were rescued. Four were killed, including the mother and the one daughter who remained behind in the hut.

It took over a year for Hannah to come to terms with the knowledge there was nothing she could have done to save the girl, but that still did not stop the guilt from overwhelming her at times. At first, Hannah battled depression and anxiety. She didn't want to be around other people and preferred spending her time either out exploring the different places her parents stopped at or just hanging with her sisters in the motor home they lived in.

Her parents talked about setting down roots and buying a house, but realized Hannah's photography and need for space was the only thing that seemed to help her. Instead, they spent more time visiting the National forests around the United States and Canada or taking scenic excursions in Europe.

It was one of their trips to South Africa that had really gotten Hannah to come out of her shell. She was eighteen and her mom had an offer to become a consultant on a new power plant under construction. They almost didn't, but Hannah wanted to see some of the wildlife there.

After several heated discussions on safety, the decision was made to go. Hannah fell in love with the open plains, rugged mountains, and even the people who seemed to thrive there. When her parents returned to the United States, Hannah decided stay.

Hannah's father was nervous, but her mom seemed to understand Hannah had finally found her way back to the living. And so, with a kiss and a promise to call frequently Hannah began using the contacts she made over the years with her photographs and writing, and began a career as a freelance photographer/writer.

She met Abasi almost two years ago during one of her many excursions into the far reaches of the plains. He had lost his wife and infant son to disease and was on a journey to join them. Instead, he found Hannah or she found him. They still argued that point.

She was taking photos of a black rhino in Kenya when they stumbled upon each other. Hannah had learned Swahili and was about to give him holy heck for ruining one of her shots when she recognized the look in his eyes as the same one she had after her kidnapping. One thing led to another and they began talking. Abasi told Hannah about the journey he was making to the other life and Hannah told him about her journey back to the living.

Hannah looked at her hands and smiled. The black rhino in the meantime was not impressed with their new found friendship. Both of them ended up in a tree.

Through the course of a night, they became friends. Abasi was determined to help Hannah learn to trust again and Hannah was determined her friend would discover he still had much to live for. Hannah chuckled when she thought back over the past two years. She still didn't trust humans. She had two new scars to prove why she shouldn't and Abasi had decided his goal in life was to find the perfect mate for Hannah. One who would overcome her distrusts and protect her, even if that meant from herself.

Hannah shook her head as she gazed back up at the stars. That was what her stupid wish had been… to find a warrior who was strong enough and brave enough and honest enough for her to trust. Personally, Hannah didn't believe any such man existed on Earth who could do that.

∽

Late the next morning, Hannah and Abasi reached another village almost fifty miles inland. Hannah waited impatiently again as the phone rang. If Tink didn't answer this time, Hannah would be on the next plane to Maine. She was just about to hang up when Tink's breathless voice came on the line.

"Hi Hannah," Tink's husky voice said.

Hannah immediately recognized the sound of *I-really-don't-want-to-talk-to-you* in it. Well, too bad. Tink was going to explain why it took her so long to answer the phone and why the hell was Hannah getting bad vibes.

"Why didn't you call me back? What is going on?" Hannah demanded in frustration. She rolled her eyes at Abasi when he raised his eyebrows. Okay, maybe demanding wasn't the best idea, but Hannah was slowly going nuts with worry.

"I'm fine, thanks for asking!" Tink replied with a grin. "I had to work today and had a bunch of errands. I was just about to call you."

"Okay," Hannah replied in frustration trying not to grind her teeth. Tink was just like their mom! Irritating and exasperating all at the same time. Hannah knew Tink was just pushing her buttons. Tink knew she wouldn't have called and left a message with RITA unless she was worried about something. "Hi Tink. How are you? I'm glad you are fine. Now, tell me what is going on. I had one of my feelings and you know they always come true."

Hannah listened as Tink drew in a shaky breath over the line. "Okay, but you aren't going to believe me," Tink said softly.

Hannah waited impatiently as Tink began telling her a story that if it had come from anyone else she would have immediately dismissed it as being ludicrous. Instead, Hannah drew in a deep breath as she realized that not only had her weird sensor been correct… the magnitude of the situation was much worse than she could ever imagine.

Tink explained how her roommate and best friend, Cosmos Raines, a resident genius on any level of the imagination had developed some type of portal… a portal that took Tink to another world. Tink explained how she had used her hammer on some type of alien creature to save a boy.

The boy turned out to be another alien, only Tink didn't realize it at first. Tink described in minute detail the spaceship she found herself on, the men she met, and how she couldn't seem to stop crying since Cosmos brought her back. Hannah listened as Tink told her about one man, a man named J'kar, who seemed to have affected her baby sister in ways neither of them understood. It took a minute for Hannah to realize Tink wasn't talking anymore.

"Hannah?" Tink asked hesitantly.

"I'm trying to decide whether I should kill Cosmos or give him a kiss for saving you," Hannah replied softly.

Hannah knew how smart Cosmos was but she never dreamed he could create something like this. The danger such a device could do to their world was unbelievable. Surely, Cosmos thought of that. As smart as he was, he should have made a list of all the things that could go wrong and had some type of safety net in place… and, what about the government? Wouldn't their government know if such a thing was possible?

Hannah would have thought Cosmos should have seen enough alien horror films growing up to know how dangerous a portal to an advanced civilization could be to their planet, not to mention the reaction if people knew life existed outside of their galaxy. Hannah believed everything Tink told her. Their father might be a science fiction writer, but Tink wasn't and she wouldn't make something like this up. If Tink said she was on a spaceship in another galaxy through a portal Cosmos built, then she was.

"I'm coming home. I'll be there as soon as I can make the arrangements," Hannah said in a voice that meant there would be no arguments. She might go ahead and kiss Cosmos while she was strangling him! Hannah thought as she began making plans in her head.

"You aren't going to tell mom, dad, or Tansy are you?" Tink asked hesitantly.

Hannah could hear the tinge of fear in Tink's voice. It wasn't that she was afraid of the others knowing… no, there was something else going on and Hannah was going to find out what it was. Besides, if Tansy found out god only knew what would happen! She would charge in guns blazing if she suspected Tink was in the remotest danger. Then, they really would have an intergalactic battle on their hands!

Now, if her folks found out that was another story! Hannah almost felt sorry for the poor aliens! Her dad would question them to death and her mom would be reinventing everything or driving them insane!

Oh, lord, thought Hannah in dismay, *it would also mean another place for her parents to get it on!*

Hannah couldn't quite suppress the shudder that escaped. That seemed to be her parent's main reason for living! Hannah groaned as she thought of all the places her parents have probably made love at or on. She had never met two hornier people in her life! Not even the animals she photographed seemed to like it as much as her parents.

Oh, God! Hannah groaned again softly. *This is so NOT what she wanted to focus on right now!*

Hannah took a deep breath. No, her parents and Tansy were not going to be informed if she could help it.

"No, at least not until I see you and determine if I need to involve them," Hannah replied gruffly. "I'll make the arrangements now and email them to you later this afternoon. Oh, it's night there, isn't it? I love you, kid. Stay safe until I get there," Hannah added distractedly. She had a lot to do if she was going to fly to Maine.

CHAPTER TWO

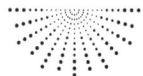

𝓑orj 'Tag Krell Manok looked at the image in his hand again. The image contained the picture of three Earth women. One was his brother, J'kar's, bond mate. The other two were her sisters. Borj had to fight off his younger brother, Mak's, efforts to steal it from him. They had finally compromised on creating a duplicate image.

It took everything inside him not to howl out in rage at the procrastination of his father and the council. He was ready to defy them all and use the portal to go find his bond mate. Borj shook his head in disbelief.

Out of all four brothers, he had always considered himself the calmest, most rational of the group. He was careful to think out every detail before executing any plan of attack. He weighed each strategy, each outcome, measuring which would benefit their people the most. That was why he was their ambassador. But right at that moment, he was anything but calm. His eyes were drawn again to the image to the left of Tink.

The female was slightly taller than the other two and had twin golden-brown braids on each side of her head hanging to her waist. She was wearing very short, tan pants ending mid-thigh, two small triangular pieces of fabric barely covered her breasts, and boots. The image was slightly wrinkled from being with Borj at all times and the corners were beginning to fray from him running his finger along the edge as if he could actually touch her delicate skin.

He knew deep down this female was his bond mate. There was no other explanation for his reaction to just the image. His brother and his bond mate, Tink, had been planet side for several days now and he was just waiting to hear of the decision as to whether he would be allowed to go and retrieve the female.

Borj glanced up when he heard his name called out. Turning, he watched as one of his father's men hurried towards him. The elderly man was breathless by the time he reached Borj. Borj waited impatiently for the man to catch his breath so he could give him the missive from his father.

"My Lord, your father and the council request your presence immediately," the man gasped out.

Borj ran his thumb over the image one more time before he nodded briskly to the man. Perhaps now he would finally get an answer to the requests he and J'kar had made for one of them to return to the female's planet.

Borj tucked the image in his breast pocket and followed his father's elderly assistant down the numerous corridors to the council chamber. As he entered, he bowed deeply to the twelve men who sat along a curved table and then again to his father who sat in the center. Straightening, he looked up and was unable to contain his surprise at the look on his father's face. Borj frowned as he approached the high table. Never had he seen his father so relaxed before.

Normally, his father was filled with barely suppressed impatience and an abundance of energy. He was known for his short temper and stern, often harsh manners. Now, while he looked impatient, it seemed for a different reason. Gone were the harsh lines of stress… in their place was a barely suppressed grin. Borj looked into his father's eyes and actually took a step back at what he saw. Was that a twinkle in his eyes? Borj shook his head. He must have finally lost his grip on reality if he thought his father had a twinkle in his eye! Perhaps he should speak to the healer…

"Borj," Teriff 'Tag Krell Manok said in a deep voice.

Borj shook his head in an effort to clear his mind and return it to the matters at hand. Bowing again, Borj replied. "My lord, you and the council requested my presence?"

"Yes. It has been brought to our attention your brother's bond mate has need of her family to be with her. The healer has mentioned this might help her during her breeding," Teriff could not keep the grin off his face as he looked around at the council members who looked at him as if they had never seen him before. "I am to be a grandfather to twins and I will not allow anything to prevent this from happening! The council has agreed with me that you should return to the female's planet and bring one of her family members back," Teriff finished, looking sternly at Borj.

Borj stared at his father for a moment as his heart leaped at the idea of bringing the female in the image back with him. He almost howled out in his excitement at the thought of seeing if the female was as responsive as his brother's mate. She would surely attach herself to him the same way his brother's bond mate did. She would be unable to keep her hands off of him. She would wrap herself around him and…

"Do you agree?" Teriff asked again.

Borj looked in confusion at his father for a moment. *What the hell did he just ask?* Borj's head was not on what his father was saying, but on the idea of burying himself balls deep inside the delicate female. Borj flushed as he realized his father and the council were waiting for his answer. Uncomfortable at asking his father to repeat his request, Borj nodded his head in agreement. The only thing he cared about was he finally had permission to return to the planet where the female he wanted lived.

Later that day, Borj looked again at the items Tink was telling him about. She was giving him so much information at such a rapid speed his head was spinning. Did she always talk so fast? The translator was having a difficult time keeping up with everything.

"These are jeans and you are wearing a T-shirt and leather jacket.

You would stick out like crazy if you wore that uniform-thingy you guys always seem to wear. We really need to get you guys some new outfits, although I have to say the form fitting on the pants is oh-la-la, if you ask me! I can always tell when J'kar is horny and the curve of his…" Tink was saying.

J'kar let out a low growl and turned Tink around rapidly in his arms, sealing his lips to hers in a deep kiss. "Enough!" J'kar growled softly under his breath. "You are…" J'kar drew in a swift breath and his face flushed as Tink turned back to Borj with a mischievous grin.

Borj bit back a groan when he saw the reason for his brother's sudden discomfort. Tink was running her hand over the hard length stretching the front of J'kar's pants though she was trying to hide it. Borj watched partly in envy and partly because he couldn't take his eyes off the erotic sight of a female responding so passionately without even having to be bitten. In all his years, Borj had never seen a more passionate female.

On Prime, females were few and far between and coupling only occurred to relieve built up aggression or to produce offspring. Before either could occur, the males would bite the females releasing a chemical into the females to increase their desire to mate. It normally required many times before the chemical would build up enough for a female to become fertile enough to receive a male's seed. Their scientists believe this might be one reason the birth rate had begun declining, especially the births of females. Another problem was only bond mated couples could reproduce.

Each Prime male and female was required to attend a Mating Ceremony when they came of age. Prime males were matched to their mates though a mating rite ceremony; and, if no match is made, life for the unattached males meant a solitary existence. The mating rites were a chemical reaction that occurred when a Prime male had a physical and emotional chemical reaction bonding them to a female. The males become overwhelmed with feelings of possessiveness, protectiveness and sexual desire.

A mating mark, a series of intricate circles denoting the unbreakable bond between mates, appears on the palm of the male and matching female when they come into contact with each other. Each mark is as individualized as the bonded pair.

The Prime, a proud warrior species, were desperate to find a species that the larger population of males could bond with. That was one of the reasons Borj had been on the warship. Borj was acting as an ambassador for Baade, their home world, hoping to find out if any of the men on board would react to the females in the nearby system. Despite meeting hundreds of females, none formed a bond mate much to the relief of some of the males on board. Many of the males had almost revolted at some of the females paraded before them.

Borj couldn't really blame them. He had fought back panic himself when presented with females who were larger than he was, had green scaly skin and far more limbs than he was comfortable with. The only other choice was one with more hair on its body than some of the creatures found on Prime. Neither represented a desirable choice. But, if it meant a bond, the male would not care what the female looked like. Borj found out his brother Mak's trip was just as unproductive.

They were returning from the nearby galaxy of Grus on a trading and fact-finding mission when they received an emergency signal from a passenger starship. The starship turned out to be a decoy to lure in unsuspecting ships. Instead of passengers, it contained a savage race of species known as the Juangans. They were a cannibalistic species known to feed on their own kind if no other food source was available.

It was on this journey that Tink suddenly appeared through a portal device created by a male of her species. Tink had saved his youngest brother, Derik's, life. When she first appeared on the bridge of the warship, all of the males were enchanted by her delicate beauty. But, it was when she touched J'kar and the mating mark appeared that all the males on the bridge realized an overwhelming hope for their future.

When the male from her world appeared on their warship and took Tink away, J'kar became inconsolable with rage and anguish. Fortunately for all of them, Tink had left two valuable pieces of her behind…RITA, the artificial intelligence program she used and a miniature portal device, both allowed them to travel to her world. Now, Borj was preparing to return to the 'warehouse' where Tink lived and meet with her friend, Cosmos. Borj had not met Cosmos yet, but between what J'kar, Brock, Lan, and Derik told him and what Tink was telling him, he felt confident he would not have any problems with the human male helping him.

"And you promise to tell Cosmos I'm okay, right?" Tink was saying.

Borj flushed as he realized he had been lost in his thoughts again. He didn't know what was wrong with him but he needed to pay better attention. He looked down at the tiny female looking up at him with her big, dark brown eyes and smiled softly.

"I promise to let him know you are well," Borj said, raising a hand to touch Tink's pale cheek. He ignored J'kar's low growl of displeasure. "I will return soon."

"With Hannah?" Tink asked with a huge grin.

Borj's eyes flashed with amusement as he glanced up at J'kar who moved closer to Tink and was drawing her back against him. "… With Hannah," Borj said softly, letting the female's name roll over his tongue.

Borj walked to the room that was now designated for traveling back and forth through the portal device. Brock and Lan were in deep discussion over a control panel. Brock looked up when Borj entered the room and nodded. Lan turned to watch as well, his eyebrows raised as he took in Borj's appearance.

"You look… different," Lan said as he let his gaze travel up and down Borj's length.

Borj grinned as he saw the skeptical look in both men's eyes. "The clothing of the human men is actually quite comfortable," Borj said.

Lan looked at Borj in amusement. "How is Tink doing? She was pleased you are going to bring her mother here?"

"Her mother?" Borj said with a frown. "I am not returning with her mother. I will bring the female called Hannah… her older sister here."

Brock burst out laughing. "Isn't that the female you and Mak were fighting over?"

Borj's frown deepened as he looked back and forth between the two men. Something wasn't right and he could tell they knew it. "The image contained all three females. Mak wants to claim the other one. I believe Tink called her Tansy. I plan to claim the one called Hannah. She is the one I am going to retrieve."

Lan was shaking his head back and forth. "Your father requested you return with the mother. Your father specifically requested she be the one brought here."

Borj grunted in frustration. "Why..." he began only to be interrupted by the man in question.

Teriff hurried into the room waving the two guards following him away impatiently. "Good. You have not left yet. I need to speak with you." Teriff glanced at Brock and Lan but did not seem concerned they were in the room.

"I want you to bring Tink's mother straight to your mother and my living quarters when you return," Teriff said in a hushed voice, looking back over his shoulder.

Borj was frowning at his father. He had never seen him this agitated before. And when did he seem so nervous about making a request before? His father was never nervous... demanding, yes... nervous never!

"I am not bringing her mother. I am bringing her sister," Borj said determinedly.

Teriff drew himself up to his full height and glared at his younger son. "No, you will bring the mother!" he demanded.

"I don't want to bring the mother," Borj said in frustration ignoring the snickering of the two men standing next to him. "I want the daughter!"

"You will bring the mother!" Teriff roared ignoring the startled looks from his son, Brock and Lan.

Borj was confused. What did it matter which family member he brought as long as he brought at least one? "But... why?" Borj asked.

Teriff flushed and looked over his shoulder again to make sure the guards were far enough away so he could not be overheard. Borj looked at the determination in his father's eyes. He was definitely missing something. Both Brock and Lan seemed to know what his father was about to say from the looks on their faces and their barely concealed attempts to keep the laughter from escaping.

"Why?" Borj demanded more forcefully.

Teriff's face turned red before he drew in a deep breath before responding. "Her mother knows all kinds of things about human females and their sexual likes and dislikes. Your mother..." Teriff couldn't keep the grin from breaking free. "Your mother has learned a lot from your brother's bond mate and she said her mother knows a lot more. Your mother demonstrated some of this new knowledge on me last night. I want her to learn more."

Borj took a step back and stared at his father in disbelief. He looked just like a young warrior having his first taste of release. Borj was already shaking his head. He was supposed to give up the possibility of a bond mate so his mother could learn better ways to pleasure his father?! Oh, Goddesses no! His father could just wait.

"No. I will bring the one called Hannah back. She is the oldest sister. She will have much knowledge and can share with mother," Borj growled out stepping up until he was almost chest to chest with his father.

Teriff raised his eyebrow at his younger son's stringent refusal. "You are refusing a direct order from your father?"

Borj gritted his teeth before nodding. "Yes," he said.

Teriff looked carefully at the determination in his younger son's eyes. Perhaps he was right. Perhaps the older sister would have just as much knowledge as the mother would. After all, it was the responsibility of the mother to pass such knowledge on to her children. Tink proved she had some of this knowledge and if the other girl was older perhaps she knew even more. Teriff frowned as he weighed which female would be more beneficial.

Borj watched as his father contemplated his refusal. Borj glanced at Lan who nodded to Brock, who slipped the portal device into Borj's hand with a small grin of encouragement. When Borj looked at both men in surprise, they just shrugged their shoulders and stepped back. Borj didn't ask twice if everything was ready. He pushed down on the top of the device and watched as a shimmering doorway appeared not two feet away from him. Teriff jerked back in surprise as Lan and

Brock each took up a position between him and the doorway leaving Borj a clear path to it.

"Safe journey, my lord," Brock said with a grin. "Bring us news of other likely females."

"... And additional images to choose from them," LAN added with a grin.

Teriff couldn't suppress his chuckle as he watched his younger son disappear through the shimmering doorway. After having tasted the delights of unrestrained... and delightfully restrained... passion, he could understand his son's resistance to his command and his eagerness to find the younger female. Teriff adjusted the front of his pants which seemed to be staying in a perpetual state of tight discomfort since he first tasted his mate's sweet essence. With a grunt to Lan and Brock for him to be notified when his son returned, Teriff decided he had worked enough for the day. He believed his mate promised him some additional lessons on how a female could receive pleasure if touched just right.

CHAPTER THREE

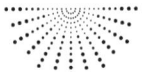

    *H*annah dropped down wearily into the chair in Tink's living room on the third floor of the warehouse. It had taken her a little over a week to get to Calais, Maine. Things had gone to hell in a hand basket almost from the moment she hung up with Tink.

One of the nice things about being in the middle of nowhere was the privacy and solitude. One of the bad things was trying to find a flight out of it. The first order was to get to a town big enough to have an airport, of any size. The closest one was over two hundred miles away as the crow flies. Unfortunately, the Land Rover didn't. So, the trip ended up being more like five hundred miles across very rugged terrain.

Three hundred miles in, the Land Rover overheated. Abasi was able to patch it to get them to another small village, but it took some creative maneuvering to get it repaired. It seemed the water pump was acting up, as well as the thermostat. There was a supply truck that came through 'sometimes' once a week. If Hannah gave a message to one of the men, he would run to the next village where another man would give the message to someone else, who would then go to another village and so on.

It took four days before she found out the truck would bring the needed parts. Normally, Hannah had some spare parts on hand, but it just so happen, the last part to break was the water pump and she forgot to get another one thinking it wouldn't go out again so soon. *And that,* she thought tiredly, *was what she got for thinking.*

Abasi, in the meantime, discovered a sudden attraction for one of the women in the village. Hannah laughed as she watched the two of them fumble around like a couple of teenagers. Even as dark as Abasi's skin was she couldn't help but tease him when he turned a brilliant red as the woman's family teased them both.

When it was time to leave, Hannah smiled at her dear friend as he promised profusely that he would return for the hand of the lovely maiden with gifts for her family in return for her hand. Hannah shook her head at how quickly they seemed to fall in love with each other. She brushed aside all of Abasi's attempts to apologize for his lack of control when they finally reached the small town where Hannah was able to hire a pilot to fly her to Cape Town.

Hannah calmly handed over the keys to the Land Rover with a kiss to her friend wishing him good luck. Abasi watched sadly as the amazing woman who became more than a friend walked away. Raising his hands to the sky, he asked the great Earth to see her safely home and grant her happiness; for if anyone deserved it, she did.

Flights from Cape Town to a variety of other cities around Europe with a multitude of layovers followed before she was finally able to get one into Bangor, Maine. Throughout it all, her internal warning system was making the Richter scale for a major earthquake look like a kiddie ride at the carnival. Hannah tried calling from every stop.

The first few days the only answer she got was from RITA saying Tink and Cosmos were not available and she couldn't tell Hannah when they would be. Hannah came to two decisions while she waited... first, she was going to short-circuit RITA the first chance she got and second she was going to beat Cosmos to within an inch of his life if someone didn't tell her what was going on! Finally, late last night Cosmos had returned her call right before she was about to board her last flight for the night. Hannah tiredly tried to remember his exact words.

"I think Tink is okay," Cosmos had replied to Hannah's question as to why Tink had not returned any of her calls.

"What do you mean... think?" Hannah had growled out so viciously several passengers sitting close to her moved away. "Where is she, Cosmos?" Hannah whispered out fiercely into the disposable cell phone she purchased.

Hannah listened in dismay as Cosmos replied he would tell her more when she arrived, but for her to try not to worry, he was working on the situation. Hannah had to hang up as the last call for boarding was being announced. *What the hell did he mean by 'he was working on the situation?'* Hannah had wondered through the entire flight across the Atlantic. An overnight stop in Philadelphia barely touched the sleep deprivation she was suffering from. Before Hannah's tired body totally gave out, she was back on a plane early this morning heading for Bangor where Cosmos picked her up.

Now, Hannah sat in the all too quiet living room of her baby sister wondering if Tink was dead or alive. Cosmos explained what happened that night over a week ago when Hannah last talked to Tink. Tink had been attacked by some senator's son. The FBI and local police were breathing down Cosmos' neck since he was the only one who was seen walking out of the equipment room where Tink and the senator's son's blood was found.

The man who was supposed to be with the senator's son had conveniently disappeared. Cosmos was released on lack of evidence that he was involved in any criminal way. He said he went to find Tink and all he found was a broken door and the blood. The waitress supported his claim he was sitting at the booth with several other men that night. Cosmos told the authorities the men were just passing through and that night was the first night he ever met them, which was the truth. He didn't tell them they were aliens from another world. No, he left that part for Hannah.

He told Hannah how Tink was critically wounded by Scott Bachman and how J'kar opened the portal to his spaceship and took Tink there, saying it was the only way to save her life. When Hannah pressed him about why it had been over a week and Tink had not returned, Cosmos simply shrugged his shoulders and looked down dejectedly saying he didn't know.

"Hannah?" Cosmos soft voice called out from the doorway. "I'm sorry."

Hannah looked up and for the first time saw the deep lines around Cosmos' mouth and his pale complexion. His eyes reflected his guilt and his worry for Tink. Hannah knew Cosmos loved Tink and would do anything to protect her. If Tink was wounded as badly as Cosmos said, his invention may be what saved her life.

"You know, mom and dad say things always turn out for the best, no matter how bad it seems at first. Maybe everything that happened was meant to be. If you hadn't invented that portal and Tink hadn't met this J'kar guy then she would be dead," Hannah said softly.

Cosmos' eyes gleamed with unshed tears at the mention of Tink being dead. "If I hadn't..."

He stopped when he saw Hannah shaking her head. "Bachman would have still targeted Tink. From the sound of it, he was already targeting her. I believe she is alive. I have to," Hannah said quietly, looking out over the river. "I can't imagine a world without her in it. Your invention brought her and J'kar together for a reason. Maybe it was to save her life. I don't know. But it was a good thing. Remember that, Cosmos. It was a good thing," Hannah repeated, looking up at Cosmos with a small smile.

Cosmos studied Hannah for a moment before he nodded. He turned to leave, but stopped for a moment before turning back around. He looked intently at Hannah before asking the question that was plaguing him.

"What does your gut tell you?" Cosmos asked hesitantly.

Hannah let a big smile slowly spread as she turned inward to see what her internal warning system was saying. "It is telling me she is not only alright but she is happy," Hannah said reluctantly. "Everything will be fine."

Cosmos' shoulders shifted as if a huge weight was lifted off of them. While he was a man of science, he also believed in Hannah's ability to sense things. He had heard too much and seen too much over the years to doubt it.

Cosmos nodded his head before replying. "Try to get some sleep. I need to go over to the university for a few hours to check on some of the equipment I've been working on. I will be taking RITA offline while I'm gone to upload some modifications I've made. Will you be okay?"

Hannah laughed tiredly. "Cosmos, I have lived in some of the most dangerous places in the world, slept with some of the most dangerous species in the world..." Hannah ignored Cosmos' raised eyebrow. She was too tired to clarify that none of them were the two-legged variety. "... And am so tired I could sleep through a major hurricane, earthquake, and tsunami without so much as a flutter of an eyelash. Go do what you need to do. We'll figure out a way to find Tink when I can think straight."

Cosmos quickly walked back into the room and gave Hannah a kiss on her nose. "See you when you wake, sleeping beauty."

Hannah hit him weakly on the shoulder before watching him head down the stairs. Forcing herself to get up, Hannah made her way into the large bathroom adjacent to Tink's bedroom. She quickly removed her clothes and climbed into the hot shower with a loud groan. *Oh, God.* Hannah thought passionately. *Hot water never felt so good!* Hot showers and soft beds were two things Hannah missed the most when she was out on one of her assignments. Within twenty minutes, Hannah was sound asleep.

～

Hannah stretched slowly several hours later. She frowned up at the ceiling, trying to orient herself. Glancing around, she remembered she was in Tink's bed in the warehouse she shared with Cosmos. Hannah lay still as she tried to figure out what could possibly have woken her from a sound sleep. She could feel that little warning siren going off that told her something wasn't quite right. It wasn't blaring like she was in danger, but it was definitely doing the 'warning... warning' message, kind of like when the National Weather Service sent out their warnings on the radio or television.

Hannah rolled out of the bed and wrapped one of Tink's robes around her. It was a bit on the small side since Hannah was a couple of inches taller than Tink's five foot four frame. Luckily, Hannah was wearing an oversized T-shirt and a pair of boxers to sleep in.

She moved quietly down the steps, her bare feet not making any noise on the oak steps. The second level of the warehouse was Cosmos' living quarters. Hannah had been in it dozens of times and quickly remembered the layout. There was a bedroom area off to the left. The stairs were to the right and across from it was the doorway to a small kitchenette area where they usually ate.

Hannah moved cautiously down the steps, the alarm sounding louder in her gut with each step she took. Hannah ducked under the stairwell and moved across through the door into the kitchenette. She reached up and took one of Tink's prized aluminum frying pans down from the hook over the center stove area and held it firmly against her chest. From the corner of her eye, Hannah saw a dark shape move against the light filtering in through the windows overlooking the river. A friend would have turned on some lights when they entered so that only left the un-friendly.

Hannah stepped back into a small recess next to the counter and held her breath. The huge figure of the intruder was moving around the open bar heading towards her. Hannah gripped the frying pan tighter and said a prayer of thanks for picking out the black silk robe instead of the hot pink one. As the figure came through the door Hannah swung with all her might bringing the bottom of the frying pan down over the back of the man's head, watching in relief as he collapsed at her feet.

∽

Borj hesitated a moment as he took stock of his surroundings. It seemed he was in some type of lab or workroom from the equipment. He didn't know what to expect when he walked through the doorway. He moved silently towards a group of what looked like primitive controls of some type. Borj ran his fingers lightly over a type of input device with strange markings on it before moving over to a set of steps leading down to a lower level.

He stopped at the top observing the strange metal archway against one wall and the cables and wires running to it. It did not appear to have an exit. Turning, he noticed a small area containing a sink and some cabinets. Out of the corner of his eye, he saw the set of clear doors Tink told him about and another set on the other side of them which she said led out of the lab.

Borj pulled the map of the warehouse out of his pocket that Tink had drawn for him and studied it carefully. Tink said if Cosmos was not in his lab he should be in his living quarters. She didn't know the exact time it was on Earth but even if Cosmos wasn't there she said Borj could wait for him on the second level.

Tink had reassured him Cosmos would know how to get in touch with Hannah if she was not there already. Borj walked over to the control panel on the wall and punched in the symbols she had written down for him. She said it was a by-pass code in case RITA was down and the person did not have voice recognition set up yet. Borj watched as the doors slid open. He stepped into the small area, turning to watch as the doors behind him closed silently. Turning back around, he entered the second set of symbols. A solid metal door clicked open and he pushed his way into a dimly lit narrow corridor. There were two sets of stairs – one led up, the other led down. Borj turned and moved upward.

At the top of the stairs the room opened up into a large area with a set of windows along one side. Borj did not know how to turn on the lighting in the area. Normally when he entered a room the lights would automatically adjust to his preferences. It didn't matter, he could see just fine with the light coming in through the windows.

He moved over to them and gazed out on the home world of the female he wanted to claim. He watched as strange transports moved back and forth over a small bridge spanning the river below him. The village below him was brightly lit with a brilliant sprinkling of lights. He could see humans walking along the edge of the river, some holding hands, others alone. He wondered vaguely if any of them could be his female. Tink said she should have arrived by now.

Borj turned away from the window and moved towards the bedroom area to see if the male was there. He walked through noticing the bed was empty and the cleansing room was dark. He returned to the living area and moved towards the food preparation area. He was curious as to how the human's living space compared with those on Baade. He had just walked into the small cooking area when he felt a sense of warning he was not alone. He was just about to turn when a blow from behind struck him and everything went dark.

∽

Hannah looked down at the figure lying face down on the kitchen floor. She quickly turned on the light over the sink and bent to make sure the man was incapacitated. Seeing he was out cold, Hannah quickly jerked open the drawers in the kitchen looking for something to tie the intruder up with. She crowed in triumph when she came across a package of plastic tie straps. *They were the large, heavy duty type too,* Hannah thought with relief.

From the size of the guy lying on the floor, she was going to need the extra strength variety. She quickly attached one to each of his wrists, then connected them together with another one. Not wanting to take a chance, she put three more around both wrists and three up his legs starting at his ankles.

Hannah stared at the three remaining ties and shrugged her shoulders. She might as well use them too. She quickly attached two more to the ties around his wrists and then to the belt loops on the back of his jeans and the last one she tied around his ankles.

Twelve of those bad boys should keep him immobile when he wakes up! Hannah thought smugly.

Hannah struggled to roll the huge male over so she could get a better look at him. She wanted to make sure she could identify him if the cops asked her. A vague thought flashed through her mind that this might be the senator's son looking for Tink, but Hannah remembered Cosmos telling her the aliens had taken him with them. *Surely, he hadn't escaped?* Hannah thought in dismay.

Hannah gasped when she got her first good look at the man under her. He was taller than Cosmos by a couple of inches and much broader. His hair was black and cut short, almost like a military style haircut. Hannah frowned as she took in his facial features. They were similar to a human's, but different somehow. He had high cheekbones but his nose was a little broader than most males. His skin color was a warm, dark tan almost like the color of a rich honey.

Hannah reached out with one of her hands and gently traced the side of his face from his hairline down to his chin. His skin felt hot against her touch. There was something different about him, but Hannah couldn't quite figure out what it was. She was just about to move away when a voice behind her made her squeal in surprise.

"What the hell are you doing?" Cosmos asked in shock.

Hannah fell back on her butt on the cold floor and grabbed her chest with her free hand. The other hand was still clutching the aluminum frying pan like a lifeline. Hannah turned enough so she could see Cosmos standing in the doorway to the kitchen that the intruder had entered through just minutes before.

"Holy crud, Cosmos! You scared the shit out of me!" Hannah gasped out.

Cosmos took in the scene in front of him. Hannah was sitting on the floor, barely covered in the robe he bought Tink last Christmas, clutching one of Tink's favorite frying pans in her hand. Next to her was a huge, unconscious male. Cosmos felt his stomach sink as he took in the man's features. If he wasn't mistaken, the aliens were back.

He let his gaze wander over the still figure frowning as he took in the odd way the man was laying with his back bowed up and his hands underneath him. As his gaze moved down, he couldn't quite hold back the small smile tugging at the corner of his lips as he noticed how Hannah had tied the poor guy up. From the guy's knees to his ankles, he had enough tie straps connected around him to hold a team of mules back. His eyes flickered to the empty tie bag lying on the floor next to the two.

"Christ, Hannah. Do you think you used enough tie straps on him?" Cosmos said shaking his head.

The figure on the floor suddenly sat up next to Hannah with a loud growl. Hannah squealed, startled at the sudden movement of the man beside her and the deep growl. Without thinking, she swung the frying pan again clobbering the man across the forehead. Both Hannah and

Cosmos watched as the man's eyes crossed for just a second before he fell backwards with a hard thump to the floor.

"Shit! You didn't kill him, did you?" Cosmos said, rushing forward to where the man was out cold again.

Hannah was trembling as she scooted back across the floor and away from the man. "I... I hope not. I didn't mean to hit him again. He... he startled me," Hannah whispered wide-eyed as Cosmos felt the man's throat and lifted up one of his eyelids.

"Do you know him, Cosmos?" Hannah whispered softly, staring at the man's chest and breathing easier as she saw it rising and falling.

"I haven't seen him, but I would bet all the equipment in my lab, he is one of *them*," Cosmos was saying as he stood up to get a pair of scissors to cut the tie straps.

"Yes, dear. He is one of them," RITA's voice came over the speaker system installed throughout the warehouse. "Boy, Hannah. You sure did a number on his head, not to mention Tink's favorite frying pan."

Hannah looked at the frying pan in confusion, then at Cosmos. "I have video surveillance throughout the warehouse, remember?" Cosmos said as he knelt down next to the still figure on the floor and began cutting the tie straps off of his legs.

Hannah nodded and bit her lip before saying tentatively. "Do you think you should be cutting all of those off?"

Cosmos looked at Hannah before glancing back down at the huge male figure on the floor. A big discolored lump was forming on his forehead. Cosmos let his gaze flicker to the frying pan Hannah was still clutching tightly against her chest. From the dents in it, he personally didn't think the guy was going to be up to moving, much less attacking anyone.

"We'll be alright," Cosmos said with a barely suppressed chuckle. Cosmos couldn't help but feel a little sorry for the aliens who were just beginning to encounter a taste of the Bell family.

CHAPTER FOUR

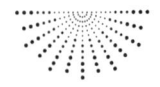

Borj groaned silently as he slowly came awake. His head was throbbing on both the front and back side. He didn't know who hit him, but whoever did was a dead man. Borj could hear a male voice talking quietly in the background. He moved one of his hands slightly and realized whoever attacked him no longer had him restrained.

That would be their fatal error, Borj thought with a grimace as another sharp stab of pain flashed through him when he moved slightly. *Because someone was going to pay for the pain he was feeling.*

Borj forced himself to remain totally still as he listened to the male's voice getting closer. He didn't react until he felt the warmth from the other body leaning over him. Moving rapidly, Borj's eyes flew open and he grabbed the large male around his throat swinging his body around at the same time, so the male was now the one lying on the floor and he was on top of him.

Borj ignored the man's yell of surprise and his choked curses. He was about to knock the man out when a sense of warning forced him to roll off the man and duck under the metal object coming towards his head. Borj was on his feet immediately and was gripping the arms of his other attacker before it dawned on him it was the image of the female he was seeking. His breath caught in his throat as he gazed down into her beautiful, dark green eyes. He was about to speak when all the air left him in a loud gush as pain exploded out of him and he dropped to his knees with a painful groan.

～

Hannah stared down at the man kneeling on the floor in front of her, his forehead lying against the cold wood. She was in the process of raising the dented frying pan above her head, to bring it back down over the back of his head again, when it was jerked out of her hands.

"You…" Cosmos said with a sympathetic look to where Borj was rocking back and forth on the floor. "… are dangerous."

Hannah looked at Cosmos in disbelief. "ME!" she screeched loudly. "He was trying to strangle you and…"

A low moan from the floor made both of them stop and look at the man who was now kneeling with his head thrown back towards the ceiling and his eyes closed. He was holding his groin protectively. "Please… for the sake of all the gods and goddesses of my world… please speak softly," he whispered hoarsely.

Borj let his eyes open slowly. Never in his life had he suffered so much from the hands of one so little. He let his gaze move from the top of Hannah's disheveled hair, down her body covered in a tiny black cloth, to her bare toes. As his gaze moved up, he was amazed his cock could respond considering how much it and his balls were throbbing at the moment.

When he grabbed Hannah's wrists to prevent her from striking him again with… his gaze flickered to the dented frying pan hanging limply from the male's hand… the cooking device, he did not expect her to react so quickly with her knee. Now, he didn't know which hurt worse: his head, his groin, or his ego. In the space of a few minutes, his tiny female had brought a Prime warrior to his knees three times.

"Oh, you poor dear, are you alright?" RITA's voice came over the speaker system sounding surprisingly like a very sympathetic Tilly Bell. "Hannah, I think the poor man could use a couple of bags of ice for his boo-boos."

Hannah rolled her eyes as she looked at Cosmos. "Did you understand a word he just said?" Hannah asked, putting one hand on her hip.

Both men's eyes moved to Hannah as the little black robe rose another notch exposing more of her creamy thigh. Borj growled low as he painfully got to his feet. His eyes swung around to glare a warning at Cosmos to redirect his eyes to another place.

Cosmos cleared his throat before smiling. It would seem this alien was staking a claim on Hannah, if he was reading the signals correctly. If that was the case, more power to him. Cosmos knew about Hannah's history and her adamant distrust of other humans, especially men. He also knew she was extremely opinionated and independent. While you could negotiate and compromise with Tink, Hannah wasn't as easy. She barely tolerated being around humans, preferring to be around the four legged types of animals or wide open spaces.

"Yes. I think his head and..." Cosmos tried to keep the grin off his face, but must not have been very successful from the glare the man sent him. "... and a few other things are hurting right now. He asked us if we could keep it down a little."

Hannah frowned at the man standing looking at her with a combination of leeriness and something else she couldn't decipher. "O...kay..." Hannah drew out as she released the breath she didn't know she was holding. "Who is he? Does he know where Tink is and if she is alright?" Hannah asked impatiently as she moved a little closer to Cosmos.

For some reason, the huge guy was freaking her out with all his staring. Not only that, her left hand was beginning to itch like mad since she touched his face! She hoped like hell the guy didn't have any type of commutable diseases or anything. Hannah stopped when the man took a step towards her with a low growl.

"Did you just growl at me?" Hannah asked in disbelief pointing to her chest. "I *know* you didn't just growl at me, you overgrown ox! So, just back off or I'll lay you out again," Hannah said as her temper flared. She held her hand out to Cosmos. "Cosmos, give me back my frying pan."

Hannah shot Cosmos a nasty glare when he pulled the frying pan she was reaching for out of her reach and hid it behind his back. She damn well wasn't going to let some alien hobnob think he could intimidate her or boss her around. She was pissed off at being woken up after only a couple of hours of sleep, scared to death thinking someone had broken in, and was worried about Tink. Now, this overgrown boar thought he could *growl* at her? *Oh, hell no.* Hannah thought as her lips tightened into a straight line and her eyes flared with hostility.

Cosmos recognized the look in Hannah's eyes and quickly stepped between the huge male glaring at her possessively and a very bad-tempered Hannah. "Go get the poor guy some ice. I think that was more of a groan than a growl. His head is probably killing him, not to mention his…" Cosmos paused when the man in front of him glared in warning. Turning, he gently pushed Hannah towards the kitchenette. "Just - go get some damn ice. PLEASE!"

Hannah let out a miffed sniff before turning and walking towards the kitchenette. The men thought she had no idea how sexy she looked with her long bare legs exposed below the tiny black, silk robe that barely covered her rounded ass. Her hips swayed seductively as she walked and her hair, which was long simply because she liked long hair, hung down her back in a tangled golden wave.

"Knock it off," Hannah called out over her shoulder, knowing perfectly well what the men were looking at.

Cosmos flushed as he turned back to the man standing next to him still staring at the doorway Hannah had disappeared through. Cosmos touched his arm to get his attention before speaking. He had a feeling it was going to be a long, long night.

"You might as well sit down. She'll be back in a minute," Cosmos said, motioning to the leather couch.

Borj's gaze flashed back to Cosmos briefly before it swung back to the doorway. He wanted to go after the female, throw her over his shoulder and return to his world where he knew she could not escape him. *Unfortunately,* he thought with a painful grimace, *he didn't think it would be as easy as that.* Instead, he moved reluctantly over to the large oversized beige couch and sat down gingerly.

"You are Cosmos?" Borj asked quietly trying not to think about the stabbing pain in his head, much less his groin, as he leaned back.

"Yes," Cosmos said, clearing his throat. "Which one are you? I've met J'kar, Derik, Lan, and Brock."

"I am called Borj. I am the second oldest. J'kar is my brother and is two planet cycles older. Derik is younger by several planet cycles," Borj said as he gently touched the knot on the back of his head. He nodded towards the frying pan Cosmos was still holding. "You will hide that thing!" he added with a thread of warning in his voice.

Cosmos laughed as he slid it under the coffee table next to the chair where he was sitting across from Borj. "Just be thankful she didn't grab the cast iron one out of the oven. You would still be out from the first time."

Both men looked up as Hannah came back into the room with a small tray. Cosmos smelled the delicious smell of fresh roasted coffee. He grinned at Hannah when he saw she had three plastic storage bags of ice, several dish towels, and a big bottle of aspirin as well. She might not like the guy, but she was a softy for anything in pain.

Hannah set the tray down on the coffee table in front of the couch, ignoring the two men staring at her and poured out three cups. She turned and handed one to Cosmos before she handed two aspirins, a cup of coffee, and one of the bags of ice wrapped in a dish towel to the huge man who was fingering the bump on his head while he watched every move she made. Hannah resisted rubbing her left hand on her thigh again as it tingled.

Since there was nowhere else to sit, she moved over to sit next to him. After all, he couldn't very well drink his coffee and hold two ice packs to his head at the same time. She definitely wasn't going to touch where the third one needed to go though she did give it to him, sort of.

"Where is Tink?" Hannah asked briskly, looking at Cosmos. She ignored Borj's wince as she dropped one ice pack on his lap while she held another ice pack to the back of his head. "When is she coming home?"

Borj adjusted the ice pack in his lap, but doubted it would cool the aching throb that filled his cock when Hannah sat down next to him on the couch. The combination of her scent and the way the robe rode up on her long legs would have made sweat bead on his brow if not for the two ice packs, one on the front and the other on the back, cooling it.

"She has recovered from her injuries," Borj said hoarsely as he felt Hannah's fingers in his short hair. *Gods,* he thought as a wave of desire washed over him, *does she not feel the same thing?*

"Thank, God!" Cosmos breathed out, relieved before he translated what Borj said for Hannah. He had been terrified even with the advanced technology of the Prime they wouldn't be able to save her after seeing the extent of her injuries.

"If she is all right then why hasn't she come back?" Hannah growled out ignoring Borj when he jerked away from her less than gentle probing.

"She cannot come. She is breeding. The healer and J'kar both fear for her and the children. They both feel she will be happier if she has a family member with her during her breeding cycle. My father and the council have agreed to let one member be brought to her," Borj said, pulling the ice pack down from his forehead. He looked Hannah in the eye so she would have little doubt as to which family member he was referring to.

Cosmos spewed coffee out and started choking when Borj said Tink was breeding. Hell, just a week or so ago, she was dying and now she was expecting a kid? Cosmos frowned. Borj had said 'children' not child.

"Breeding?" Hannah asked, dazed when Cosmos translated the last part. Her baby sister was pregnant? Already? By some alien dude?

"What the fuck do you mean by breeding?" Hannah asked at the same time Cosmos choked out "children?"

Borj grinned with pride. "She is expecting what you call 'twins.' Our people have never heard of having more than one child at a time. Tink called J'kar a 'potent son-of-a-bitch'. My father wishes, among other things, for all of his sons to be this," Borj said with a devilish gleam in his eye as he stared at Hannah.

~

It was close to two o'clock in the morning when Hannah finally told Cosmos she was done… finished… totally fried. She couldn't handle anything else unless she got some serious sleep. While she didn't understand a word coming out of Borj's mouth, she did understand the look in his eyes and the language in his body.

She had photographed enough animals mating in the wild, not to mention having two very horny parents growing up, to get the message loud and clear he wouldn't mind sharing a bed with her. Borj had not been happy when Cosmos let him know he would not be joining Hannah upstairs.

Hannah laid in the dark waiting for her overtired mind to finally calm down enough for sleep to overtake her. She absently ran the fingers of her right hand over the palm of her left. She had noticed when she was making the coffee earlier in the kitchenette downstairs that a series of circles forming a pattern had appeared in the center of her left palm. She didn't want to say anything in front of Borj about it.

Unfortunately, she never got a chance to be alone with Cosmos after their unexpected visitor woke up. Hannah frowned as she remembered every time Cosmos got too close to her, Borj would start doing his growling thing again. It was beginning to piss her off. He was acting like some dog in a pissing contest or, she thought with a grin, that big-ass lion she was photographing with the ladies.

Hannah shivered as a sense of forewarning ran through her that her life was about to change – big time – and she wasn't going to have a lot of say about it. Rolling over, she punched the pillow and forced her mind to think of other things than big, sexy aliens with beautiful silver eyes. Her fingers, though, had a mind of their own as they continued to stroke the circles softly.

Borj let out another soft groan as he turned on the oversized couch. Sweat was beaded on his forehead and he was in pain. This time, however, was for an entirely different reason. He could feel each stroke of Hannah's fingers as if she were touching his overheated skin.

He noticed the mating mark almost immediately when he sat down. He had felt a strange tingling and burning sensation and had almost been too nervous to look. He remembered J'kar telling him of how it felt when Tink and he touched for the first time... as if an electrical charge had burned its way through his body.

Borj bit back a painful chuckle as he rolled over onto his back trying to find a place where the bump on the back of his head wouldn't cause discomfort. He, unfortunately, had been unconscious during their first touch. Borj grinned as he thought of how spirited his bond mate was before it dissolved to a frown at how dangerous it could have been if it had been someone else other than him in the warehouse.

He needed to return with Hannah to his world. He needed to finish the mating rite ceremony. Borj felt the ache deep inside as he fought the desire to claim his mate. The chemical reaction between the two of them started the moment they touched.

When his body, even in his unconscious state, found the perfect chemical balance with Hannah's he was destined to claim her as his own. His body hardened even more as a wave of sexual desire flowed through him. Borj gritted his teeth and wondered how J'kar was ever able to leave his bond mate's side. He had thought Hannah beautiful from just the image he had but seeing her, touching her skin, and scenting her delicate fragrance was enough to drive him insane with need.

Borj realized if he did not relieve some of the pressure building inside him he would never be able to rest. Sitting up, he bit back a moan as his cock protested its confinement within the tight pants human males called jeans. The 'zipper' on it was biting into his flesh. He couldn't help but feel sorry for the males if this is what they had to suffer. Borj moved quietly across the floor until he came to the room containing a 'toilet' and a sink. Cosmos referred to it as a 'half-bath'. It was small but it would meet Borj's needs for the moment.

Softly closing the door, Borj touched the switch to illuminate the room. Standing in front of the sink, he lowered the zipper and unbuttoned the fastener holding his pants on. Borj gritted his teeth and closed his eyes against his image being reflected in the mirror.

Instead, he brought up Hannah's beautiful face. He pictured her with her hair as it was earlier flowing down her back. As he gripped his cock, he imagined it was her soft hands wrapped around him.

He smiled at the thought of slowly removing the tiny black piece of cloth and watching as it slid off her pale, creamy shoulders. He would run his tongue over the curve of them, tasting each delectable inch as he worked his way down to her full breasts. He knew she had nipples from the information Tink related during her lesson on oral sex. He remembered in the vidcom she talked about how sensitive a human female's breasts were and how a man sucking on them could cause her to have an orgasm if he did it right.

Borj groaned louder as he pumped his cock thinking about Hannah doing oral sex on him as Tink described. The thought of her beautiful lips wrapped around him caused him to bite back a loud groan as he came in the sink. Borj's head fell forward as hot stream after hot stream of his seed poured out. He leaned his right palm against the sink while he let his left hand continue to gently run up and down the length of his cock until it became so sensitive it was painful to the touch.

Taking a deep breath, he opened his eyes and stared at his reflection in the mirror. His dark silver eyes had twin flames of desire and determination burning deep inside them. The next time he sought release it would not be his hand that gave it to him, he swore darkly.

CHAPTER FIVE

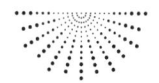

Hannah woke late the next day. She rolled over onto her back and sighed as she remembered her last thoughts before she had fallen into the deepest, most restful sleep she had ever had. Hannah flushed and moved restlessly against the sheets as she remembered the very vivid dream she had before exhaustion, and something else, claimed her.

Sitting up in bed, Hannah shook her head at how real dreams could be. She could have sworn Borj touched her in ways she had never let a man near enough to do. She let her hands move to her breasts surprised to find them sensitive and tender to her touch.

Maybe I'm getting ready to start, she thought vaguely.

Frowning, she pushed the covers back and climbed out of the bed determined to dismiss the erotic dream for what it was – a dream. She was not about to let any male, alien or not, near enough to hurt her! Hannah knew it was irrational to be afraid of being intimate with another person, but it was her irrationality.

She learned to live with it a long time ago when she would break out in sweats every time a guy would come near her. She also knew deep down that was why she worked as far away from others as possible. It was just safer not to care.

Pushing the bad thoughts out of her head, she was almost to the door of the bathroom when she heard her name called out. Turning, she smiled at Cosmos standing in the doorway trying not to cuss as he straightened the flower vase that kept falling over on the tray. Hannah leaned back watching as one of the smartest men in the world fumbled with trying to carry a tray without dropping it. She finally felt so sorry for him she couldn't help but walk over and pluck the flower – vase and all – off the tray.

Cosmos gave Hannah a crooked grin. "Thanks! I wanted to surprise you with brunch in bed. I also thought I might be able to talk to you alone for a few minutes before Borj comes storming in here," Cosmos said following Hannah over to the bed where he set the tray down with a sigh of relief.

Hannah laughed as she picked up a piece of the buttered toast and took a bite. "Is he giving you problems this morning?" she asked, amused sipping at the coffee with a sigh.

Cosmos laughed as he rubbed the back of his neck. "You could say that. But, I took care of it. I gave him a stack of Playboy and Penthouse magazines, among others, to look at. You should see his face. Something tells me they don't have those on his planet."

Hannah paused in the process of taking another bite of the toast and raised an eyebrow. The warning bells were starting again. "Okay, out with it. What is wrong?"

Cosmos looked at Hannah a moment before sighing deeply. He really, really didn't think she was going to like what he had to say. Especially, if what Borj showed him and told him was true. He halfway wondered if it would be safer to stand, but Hannah took that option out of the picture when she set the toast down and grabbed his chin turning it towards her.

"What is wrong?" Hannah repeated in her no-nonsense voice.

"Can I see your hands for a moment?" Cosmos asked suddenly.

Hannah jerked back and rubbed both her palms on her thighs. "Why?" she asked suspiciously.

Cosmos' face darkened as he realized everything Borj told him was true. The same thing that happened to Tink was happening to Hannah.

It was all his damn fault for inventing that double-damn gateway! Cosmos thought in dismay.

"Let me see them," Cosmos asked quietly.

Hannah's hands trembled as she slowly extended them until they lay palm down in Cosmos' huge ones. Cosmos squeezed them briefly before turning them over so he could see her palms. Sure enough, she had a series of intricate circles forming a pattern in the center of her left palm. Cosmos knew that when he scanned it, it would match perfectly with the one on Borj's left palm. They were bond mates.

"I'm a what?" Hannah whispered in disbelief.

Cosmos flushed when he realized he had spoken aloud. "You are Borj's bond mate. He said in his world when a male and a female are compatible for reproducing they are bond mates." Cosmos ran his hand through his hair again before he frowned. "No, that's not exactly right. Let me try this again.

All males and females go through a mating rite ceremony to determine who they will mate with. If the mating mark, the circles on your palm, appear then the match is good and they can reproduce. If no mark appears, they wait and do it again at the next ceremony unless they happen to meet before, which is rare as the females are not let out of their 'houses' alone often as a way of protecting them from any males who may have become more aggressive due to not having a mate. Is this making any sense?" Cosmos asked, looking at Hannah for the first time since he saw the patterns on her palm.

Hannah's horror at what Cosmos was saying was growing beyond anything she had ever felt before. This alien guy thought she was his mate because a bunch of circles had appeared on her hand? The circles were a get straight to the baby making stage? Is this what happened to Tink? She was kidnapped so she could become a breeding mare? He expected her to be caged in some 'house' all the time and just be there whenever he... whenever he... Hannah's mind revolted at the next step.

"Hannah, are you okay?" Cosmos was saying.

Cosmos saw Hannah pull back away from him and sway slightly as if she had just received a huge shock. He was concerned as the color slowly faded from her face, leaving her very pale and shaken. He quickly pulled the tray off the bed and set it on the floor before turning back to gather Hannah tightly in his arms.

"I can't do it," Hannah was saying softly under her breath over and over. "Get it off me, Cosmos. I can't have it on me."

Cosmos was concerned as Hannah's voice started to get louder and sounded more than a little hysterical. "Get it off of me, Cosmos. NOW! Get it off of me!"

"Hannah… I'll try," Cosmos said quietly realizing Hannah was on the verge of a total meltdown.

Hannah turned her blank stare to him. "You have to do it, Cosmos. I won't be his or anyone else's. It would kill me to be locked up. I… I don't want anyone touching me like that… like they did those other women… I… I can't do it. You have to help me, Cosmos," Hannah whispered faintly.

~

It took Cosmos another ten minutes to get Hannah to believe his promise to try to undo the mating mark. He walked down the steps slowly. Hannah had finally gone into the bathroom to get cleaned up. He hoped she would be in a better mood when she was done.

Cosmos hadn't been there when Hannah had been kidnapped, but he knew it had been bad… very bad. From what Tink told him, Hannah didn't talk much after the incident. Tink told him Hannah would just sit and stare out the window for hours, not moving from the seat as they rode down the road, not talking, not doing anything.

When they would stop, she would often go off alone. Tink really didn't know what happened just that Hannah had escaped the kidnappers and spent ten days in the jungle. Her parents never talked about it with her or Tansy. They said it was at Hannah's request that they didn't.

"She is awake?" Borj asked, looking up from the magazine he was looking through.

Cosmos couldn't help the small grin that curved his lips. In order to get a few minutes alone with Hannah, Cosmos had dug out his teenage collection of Penthouse, Playboy, and Sports Illustrated Swimsuit edition magazines. He may have been shy around the girls, but that didn't mean he didn't like to look at them. Borj had never seen anything like them and Cosmos couldn't help but laugh as he eyes got bigger and bigger with each edition. Borj didn't even realize Cosmos was gone until he came back down.

Borj was frowning as he looked at one centerfold. "My Hannah is not in any of these, is she? I would have to kill you and every male who looked at her otherwise," Borj said, holding the picture of Miss November up.

Cosmos bit back a laugh. "No, I really don't think you will find Hannah in any of those types of magazines. I do have a few magazines that you will find her in, though," Cosmos added mischievously.

Borj's head jerked up and his face darkened threateningly. "Show me!" he gritted out between his teeth.

Cosmos opened a cabinet that contained Tink's collection of her sister's work. Wildlife, Times, National Geographic, WWW, and others contained pictures and articles about Hannah from the time she was six until her most recent interview last year after she was wounded when one of the countries she was in exploded with violence. She won international recognition with her depiction of the damage done to humans, wildlife, and the environment.

Cosmos set the magazines down in front of Borj and watched him carefully as he opened each magazine. He wanted to see Borj's reaction to Hannah's work. It was obvious her love of the outdoors and her compassion for the things she photographed.

Borj felt a wave of fury flood him when Cosmos first told him Hannah was in a 'magazine'. Since the documents Cosmos gave him first were his only experience with human media, he thought they would all be the same. But, the images he was looking at now took his breath away. He looked at the pictures Cosmos explained Hannah took.

There was a family of huge, black hair creatures grouped together in what looked like a dense jungle. One creature had a blaze of silver across its back and was studying the smaller group. Another showed large herds of another creature jumping through the water while huge predators grabbed for them. Each was more spectacular than the next.

When Cosmos handed him another article, he saw Hannah and a dark-skinned male standing next to each other smiling.

"That's Abasi. He works with Hannah when she does her African shoots," Cosmos was saying.

Borj nodded, not feeling threatened as he could see the love in the male's eyes, but nothing stating he was possessive of Hannah. Borj made a choked sound when he came to the pictures of some of the atrocities Hannah photographed. The next few photographs on the opposite page were not Hannah's but of Hannah. The male, Abasi, had his arms around her and she was covered in blood.

"Tell me what this says," Borj choked out as he ran his finger over the photograph of Hannah's face lined in pain. He let his finger run down to the image of her shirt, torn with blood coating the front.

Cosmos cleared his throat as he read the caption under the photograph.

Internationally Renowned Wildlife Photographer Wounded

Hannah Bell, an internationally award winning wildlife photographer was wounded during a recent revolution in Chad. Bell, known more for her photographs of endangered species, brought world-wide attention to the atrocities of certain rebel groups. The photograph above shows Bell, with her guide, being helped after rebel groups wounded her.

Borj looked at the photograph, but his mind was elsewhere. This was a very dangerous world for females. How could the males let the females do anything so dangerous? Why did her family not prevent her from going to these places unprotected?

"Females are different here, Borj. You can't cage a girl like Hannah up. If you do, it would kill her," Cosmos said, responding to the questions Borj muttered under his breath. He knew he had to get Borj to understand this or it could have devastating effects on both of them. "She is like the wild creatures she photographs. They need the freedom to roam. Hannah… Hannah's been through more than any girl should ever go through. When she was fifteen something really bad happened to her that changed her life. She…" Cosmos' voice faded when Borj suddenly jerked up off the couch heading for the stairs.

Borj felt a shiver of apprehension go through him. He was listening intently to what Cosmos was saying when a sudden shaft of pain flashed through his left palm. Borj drew in a deep breath and clenched his fist against the pain as it spread up his arm. He focused inward briefly and Hannah's image rose before him.

Borj jerked off the couch and moved rapidly up the stairs, taking them three at a time. He burst into the upper living area and continued through until he was in front of the bathroom. Borj didn't pause as he hit the door with his hand, breaking the latch. He stood breathing heavily through his nose in an effort to push the pain radiating up through his left arm away. He stared in horror at Hannah, who was leaning over the edge of the bathroom sink, a sharp cutting tool in her hand. His gaze followed the tiny flow of blood down the sink from where her left hand lay against the edge.

~

Hannah stood under the flow of the hot water as long as she could, letting all the things Cosmos told her run through her mind over and over. It wasn't until she was shaving her legs that she got the idea that maybe she could scrape the circles off of her hand. After all, it didn't look like it was that deep. It was worth a try.

It was ridiculous to think a bunch of circles popping up on someone's hand meant you were mated to them. Yes, she had seen some of the mating rituals of different tribes around the world that used unusual ways to bind a couple but she personally didn't believe in it. Hell, even wedding rings were a ritual, but you could still take them off. There had to be a way to remove them. The first thing she tried was scrubbing it with a fingernail brush and soap. All that did was cause it to become more sensitive.

Hannah turned off the shower and quickly dried and dressed in a pair of loose fitting cargo pants and a forest green T-shirt. She didn't bother with putting on any shoes. She flipped her head over and brushed the long length out before she divided it into three sections and braided it. Looking in the mirror, she could still see the dark shadows under her eyes from not getting enough rest.

Hannah shrugged. *The rest could come later. Right now, get rid of the circles, then find Tink.*

Hannah pulled a new razor blade out of the cartridge container and carefully pulled it apart so she had just one of the super sharp blades. Bending at the sink, she gently began scrapping a small section of her left palm where the edge of the circles began. She frowned when nothing seemed to happen. Maybe it was a little deeper than she thought. She knew some parasites burrowed under the skin. Hannah decided she would try to cut a small section out.

Hannah bit her lip as she felt the first slice break through the skin. It wasn't like she had never needed to cut on herself before. She was used to having to remove thorns or lance areas where some type of critter had bitten her so she could release the poison. The moment she sliced through the first circle pain exploded throughout her arm and down through her body.

Hannah bit back the surprised cry at how much it hurt. Blood welded up from the small cut and began dripping down through her fingers. Hannah laid her palm over the edge of the sink so the blood would drain down it. Holding her breath, she moved the razor blade in her trembling right hand back over the circle to try again when the door to the bathroom suddenly exploded inward.

Hannah stared in shock as an enraged Borj looked from her bleeding palm to the razor in her right hand. "What in the *hockta balmas*, are you doing?" Borj asked furiously.

"What?" Hannah asked, dazed as her palm pulsed. "What are you doing in here?"

"Hannah?" Cosmos asked from behind Borj. Hannah heard his gasp as he saw what she was doing. "What the fuck are you doing?"

"I…I wanted to see if I could scrape the circles off," Hannah explained, looking back and forth between the two men. Why were they acting like she had done something horrific? It was her stupid hand.

Borj growled out and stomped forward, gripping her right wrist hard enough to make her drop the razor blade. Hannah's protest died on her lips when he grabbed her left wrist and raised her palm to his mouth. He gently ran his tongue over the small cut. Hannah immediately noticed the pain faded and warmth began seeping up through her arm into the rest of her body. She moaned softly as Borj continued to lap at the tiny wound.

Borj closed his eyes as the sweet taste of Hannah flowed over his tongue. *Hockta balmas, hell's balls but she tasted delicious.* He opened his eyes to stare down into the beautiful dark green eyes of his mate. He pulled both of her arms up and around his neck before he grasped her around her slim waist, lifting her until she was sitting on the edge of the counter by the sink. He refused to release her gaze as he slowly lowered his head. He paused for just a moment to see if she would pull away and gave a small sigh of thanks when instead, she leaned forward touching his lips tentatively with her own.

CHAPTER SIX

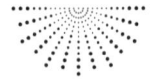

Hannah trembled as she pressed her lips lightly against Borj's firm ones. It was the last thing she could ever have imagined herself doing, but it just felt right. She remembered her mom telling her once after one of her panic attacks that when the right guy came along her body might recognize him before her mind did. Right now, her mind was lost in a haze of desire.

Hannah let her fingers slowly move over Borj's broad shoulders to skim lightly along the back of his neck before she let her fingers bury themselves in his short hair. Hannah felt the slight increase in pressure against her lips as Borj pressed deeper, wanting her to open for him. Her arms tightened around him and her hands gripped the back of his head preventing him from pulling away as she opened her mouth enough to let the tip of her tongue trace along his.

Borj felt a wave of tenderness flood him at the tentative touch of Hannah's lips. She reminded him of some of the Ta'caras, a small furry creature found deep in the forest of their world. It was extremely rare to see one for they were very shy and cautious. Their fur was extremely soft and warm. They were hunted almost to extinction many generations ago. Hunting them became unlawful after the ruling council determined there was no longer a need for their fur. Even so, the cost of those times still weighed on the creatures and they seldom came out in the open, preferring the dense forests instead.

Borj wrapped his arms tighter around Hannah as she pressed closer to him. Instinctively, he knew she needed to be the one in control right now. He needed to let her set the pace if she was to begin to trust him. It about killed him to not take her, possess her like his instincts told him to. He wanted to bite her, to seal her to him both physically and emotionally, but he knew to do so now would have devastating consequences if she did not learn to trust him first.

Borj shuddered at the first touch of Hannah's tongue against his lips. Borj pressed deeper letting Hannah's tongue bridge the gap between them making them one. His arms tightened even more, crushing her breasts against his chest and causing a painful groan to escape as the need to claim her filled his cock until it was straining against the confines of his pants. Is this what his brother felt when he was with his bond mate? To have a female respond without the need for stimulus from the chemicals in his bite was more arousing than anything he had ever experienced before. Never in all his years did he ever expect for a female to respond with unrestrained passion.

The sound of a throat clearing behind them finally filtered through Hannah's brain. Pulling back, she let her hands drop to Borj's shoulders. Hannah let her head drop until her forehead rested against his right shoulder. She used the brief respite from looking at Borj to attempt to get her raging hormones back under control.

"Wow," Hannah murmured just soft enough for Borj to hear.

Borj chuckled as he wrapped his arms tighter around Hannah drawing her close against the warm strength of his body. "I do not know this word, but I think I agree."

Hannah looked up puzzled at Borj not understanding what he said. "Huh?"

Borj closed his eyes in frustration. He needed to implant the translator he brought with him. Borj turned to Cosmos who was staring at Hannah with a bemused expression on his face.

"I have a translator I brought for Hannah. Can you ask her if it would be permissible to her to implant it so she may understand what I am saying?" Borj asked Cosmos.

"Uh, sure. Hannah?" Cosmos said from the doorway. "Borj has a translator like they put in me. He wants to know if he can implant one in you so you can understand him. It doesn't hurt. Hell, I didn't even know they did it. It takes a little while though to get used to the words coming out of their mouths and the words forming in your head to sync, though."

Hannah looked at Cosmos doubtfully for a moment before nodding. It would help if she could understand everything that was going on and not have to rely on Cosmos to translate. After all, some things do get lost in translation. She had learned that the hard way more than once.

"Okay," Hannah said, looking at Borj for the first time since kissing him.

Borj smiled tenderly and brushed a stray strand of hair back behind her ear. He loved the way her cheeks warmed to a light pink color at his touch. He reached into the front pocket of his pants and pulled out a small square container about the size of a dime. Hannah watched as he pushed a small button and the box transformed into a long, skinny cylinder with a tiny dot that shimmered like a diamond in the bathroom light. Borj gently cupped Hannah's chin, turning it so he could place the device in her ear. Hannah felt a brief rush of air, then nothing. Borj turned her head the other way and did the same thing to her other ear.

"Having a translator in both ears will make it easier for you, *ku lei*," Borj said softly against her ear.

Hannah's eyes widened as she gasped. She understood what he just said. He called her 'my beloved'.

~

"So, tell me about your world?" Hannah asked several hours later as she sat curled up on Cosmos' couch. Borj was sitting next to her while they waited for Cosmos to come back upstairs. He was checking some updates in his lab.

After Borj implanted the translator into Hannah's ears RITA came over the intercom system to let them know they had a visitor at the door. RITA ran a security check and informed Cosmos and Hannah the visitor was a private detective hired by Senator Bachman. By the time Cosmos got to the downstairs entrance way, he knew the man's life history.

Borj listened in, impressed with RITA's thoroughness and her somewhat amusing suggestions should the man become less than pleasant. Cosmos refused to let the man beyond the entrance foyer. He answered all the man's questions, repeating verbatim the same answers he gave the FBI and local police. Hannah had to hold Borj back when the man threatened Cosmos if he refused to let him look around the warehouse.

Since neither the FBI nor the police could obtain a search warrant due to lack of evidence, Cosmos was not concerned. Even if they were able to get one, they wouldn't have found anything. Cosmos had set up safety protocols with RITA to delete all files and erase the programming for the gateway should anyone try to access it without his authorization. That was one of the reasons RITA had been offline when Borj showed up.

Borj couldn't resist touching Hannah at every opportunity. He bit back the small smile of satisfaction as he noticed that every time he touched her, she seemed to let his hand stay a little longer before pulling away. It would take considerable restraint on his part and a lot of patience, but he was determined she would grow to trust him.

"My people are called the Prime. We are a proud warrior people who live in a galaxy that has several habitable planets," Borj answered as he wound a long strand of Hannah's hair that had come loose around one of his fingers. "There are three planets in the Prime system that can support life comfortably. Only one is fully inhabited, though.

My planet is called Baade. It is the home world of the Prime. There are two smaller planets, Lacertae and Carafe, as well. They are small and used primarily as cargo ports, mining facilities, and military. Our most important resource is base crystals. It is used to help power our world and our warships," Borj said distractedly as the silky strand he was playing with caressed the circles against his left palm.

"You are so beautiful. I can't wait to claim you as my own," Borj thought

as he watched the colors in her hair dance as the sunlight from the windows hit it.

"What the..." Hannah jerked in surprise as she heard Borj's voice in her head.

Borj's own eyes widened as he realized the bond was getting stronger. He knew that in bond mates a telepathic link developed between the male and the female. This evolved as a way for the males to protect their mates from other males who might try to take or harm them. He had never heard of it forming without the mating ceremony being complete and the male's claim on the female sealed through his claiming of her.

"You can hear me?" Borj thought cautiously.

"I can hear him in my mind," Hannah thought at the same time as she nodded her head. "What... what's going on?"

Borj was unable to resist pulling Hannah over onto his lap and crushing his mouth down onto hers in a passionate kiss. There was no denying she was his bond mate. *Their bond must be incredibly strong for them to be able to communicate like this before his claiming,* Borj thought in awe.

"God, you two need to get a room," Cosmos said breaking the mood.

Hannah flushed a deep red and scrambled off of Borj's lap. She moved away from Borj to stand next to the bank of windows overlooking the river and turned her back to both men. Hannah muttered a curse as she straightened her shirt with a frown.

"When did it ride up?" she wondered.

"I think when my hand was moving towards your breast," Borj replied with a chuckle.

"Stop that!" Hannah said crossly looking over her shoulder at Borj who just grinned at her.

"Stop what?" Cosmos said, looking back and forth between Hannah and Borj.

"He's talking in my head now," Hannah said with a pout towards Borj. Turning, she looked at Cosmos with a determined expression on her face. "Cosmos, you said you would try to see if you could get rid of the circles on my hand. What are you planning to do?"

Borj surged off the couch with a low, dangerous growl. Hannah squealed as Borj wrapped his arms around her. She didn't even see him move! Borj jerked Hannah up against his body holding her tight and turned so that his body was between her and Cosmos.

"Never!" Borj snarled in a deep voice. "She is mine."

"Whoa! Calm down, man. I won't touch her," Cosmos said with a laugh.

"COSMOS! You promised!" Hannah cried out as she tried to wiggle out of Borj's arms. "You…" Hannah's words ended in a gasp as her lips were covered by a set of very determined ones.

"Never, Hannah. Never can you break our bond," Borj said fiercely.

"Come on, guys! Give a guy a break! I haven't been laid in almost six months and you two are making it really, really difficult here," Cosmos complained as he threw up his hands in frustration.

Hannah jerked back and looked at Cosmos in shock. "That is *way* too much information for me, Cosmos!"

Cosmos grinned before replying. "Yeah, I know. But I figured it might douse the flames burning in here."

Borj shook his head as he looked at Cosmos. "Is he always like this?"

"Unfortunately, I've seen him worse," Hannah replied, relaxing in Borj's arms.

Borj let Hannah slide down his body, making sure she could feel his body's reaction to her. He knew the minute she felt his arousal by the way she froze and a wild, panicked look came into her eyes. Borj frowned when he felt Hannah's hands immediately go between them and she pushed herself back away from him.

"It is *so* not going to happen," Hannah hissed out in a low voice at him.

Borj's eyes lit with determination. Bending forward until his mouth was almost touching hers again, Borj whispered back huskily. "Yes, it is."

"Cosmos, there is someone else at the door," RITA's voice came over the line. "Oh! It's Tilly and Angus! Land sakes, I wasn't expecting them."

Hannah groaned out loud at the same time as Cosmos did. "You have to hide him," Hannah said frantically as she started pushing Borj towards the stairs leading to Tink's living quarters. "You have to hide! If my parents see you there will be no end to the questions."

Pushing Borj was like pushing a solid concrete wall. He wouldn't budge. "Come on, you have to move, dammit. Faster!" Hannah said desperately.

"She's right, Borj. If Tink's mom and dad get a look at you, it is all over, man," Cosmos said, grabbing Playboy and Penthouse magazines and shoving them under the cushions of the couch, under the couch itself, and in the drawer of the coffee table. He was shoving them anywhere he could with the hope that Tink's parents wouldn't see them. God, he was feeling like when he was a teenager again!

"RITA, don't you dare let them in yet!" Hannah called out over her shoulder as she dragged a reluctant Borj behind her.

"Sorry, dear. I already did. They are headed up the stairs. But don't worry, the stairwell is kind-of dark and I think your dad just grabbed your mom's butt. The heat signatures are definitely increasing!" RITA said with a chuckle.

"Oh God! Talk about too much information," Hannah groaned. "When are they ever going to get enough of each other?"

Cosmos picked up a stack of Sports Illustrated magazines and thrust them under some of the wildlife magazines laying on the end table. "Knowing your folks… never. Even I don't know how your dad does it at his age and I'm the scientist of the bunch," Cosmos called out as he picked up the empty cups, plates, and plastic bags filled with water from the melted ice and hurried to carry them into the kitchen. "Go hide him. I'll try to distract your folks for a little while."

Hannah yanked on Borj's arm trying to get him to move faster. He really, really didn't understand how serious this was. If her parents discovered there was an eligible man besides Cosmos in the same building as Hannah, she was doomed. They would have her married to him by this afternoon! Her parents had both made up their minds that it was high time Hannah worked through her phobia of men and relationships.

For the past three years her mom regularly sent her emails of matchmaking web sites, emails of eligible male children of their friends, and even hired a relationship advisor for Hannah. That was the number one reason she had avoided her family for the past two years. Her mom was worse than a dog in a dinosaur exhibit. She would have made T-Rex sit down and weep. But, if you threw her dad into the mix as well…Hannah shuddered and looked at Borj who had an amazingly cute look of pure confusion on his face.

"Why are you so frightened of your parents? Do they hurt you? Tink seemed to think your parents were wonderful? Did they not love you?" Borj asked confused.

"Ohhh, be quiet! I don't want them to hear you," Hannah whispered fiercely pushing Borj further into Tink's living area and looking down the stairs fearfully. "If they see you, especially the way you look at me, we'll be married before the end of the day! My parents want me to meet a guy so badly they've thrown every Tom, Dick, and Harry in my face," Hannah muttered peering down the staircase and listening as Cosmos talked to her dad.

"You mean if your parents see you with me they will want me to claim you?" Borj asked quietly, looking intently at Hannah's flushed face as she looked around the corner of the staircase.

"Yes," Hannah whispered distractedly.

She was really trying to hear what was being said. Maybe her parents wouldn't even know she was here. Maybe she would get a break. She could get Borj to bring Tink back and get out before her parents realized she was back in the States.

"They would insist if one of these men looked at you and touched you that you must bond with them?" Borj asked as his eyes began to flame again and his mouth began to curve into a wicked smile.

"Are you kidding? If my folks found out you were a horny alien here to kidnap me they would probably – no definitely – get you the rope to tie me up! This is worse than any TV reality show," Hannah hissed out under her breath as she shooed with her hand for him to back up.

"I…" Hannah's voice faded as she got a look at Borj's face. "Oh, no…. oh, no… you are *so* not going to do what I think you want to. If you thought last night hurt you haven't felt anything yet," Hannah said, pushing herself against the wall and trying to scoot around Borj.

"I will take my chances," Borj said as he reached for her.

"Uh, Tink isn't here right now. I know she is going to be upset at missing you. She, uh, she went out of town for a while," Cosmos said, looking up at Angus Bell with what he hoped was a convincing face.

"Oh, dear. I knew we should have called first," Tilly said, looking around with a frown.

Cosmos bit back a curse when Tilly walked over and pulled one of the Penthouse magazines out from under the sofa cushion. Her eyes widened with delighted interest and she turned and sat down on the sofa. Cosmos was turning back to Angus when a loud scream followed by a stream of curses filled the air from above them.

"I thought Hannah was here," Tilly said calmly as she leafed through the magazine turning it this way and that way at times.

Cosmos' closed his eyes, listening at the sound of grunts and alien curses coming down the stairs. Cracking his eyes open, he watched as Borj fought to keep from getting his nose busted. His shins were not as fortunate. Cosmos grimaced as another flash of pain crossed Borj's face.

"Let me go, you jerk!" Hannah yelled. "I am so going to beat the crap out of you."

Borj grunted as the back of Hannah's head connected with his chin. He felt the taste of blood as his lip connected with his teeth. His mate was a blood-thirsty little thing. Borj tightened his arms around her effectively trapping her arms against her side. He should have thought about tying her feet though. Borj groaned as the thought of having Hannah tied up in his bed drew vivid pictures in his mind.

"You can just keep dreaming, buddy! It will be a cold day in hell before I let you tie me up!" Hannah growled out trying to reach around far enough to bite him.

"Oh dear, Angus, I think I love him already. What do you think?" Tilly Bell's lilting voice chuckled out.

Angus looked at his wife who had a picture of Miss June opened up on her lap. He leaned down over the couch and brushed a kiss across her neck. Tilly tilted her head to the side to give him better access with a low moan.

"I think Miss June has nothing on you, my love," Angus said with a quiet growl.

"Oh. My. God!" Hannah cried out furiously. "Hello! Your oldest daughter is getting attacked... manhandled... kidnapped... can't you at least act like you give a damn?"

Tilly looked over her shoulder. Her breath caught in her throat as she stared intently at the huge male holding her struggling oldest daughter against him. He was breathtaking. And, he had Hannah. He was absolutely perfect! Tilly laid the magazine down on the coffee table and stood up so she could get a better look at the man.

"Angus," Tilly said softly.

Angus was doing some staring of his own. The moment he saw the silver flames burning in the man's eyes he knew he wasn't human. Hell, he wrote about aliens every single day. He knew what a human looked like, but he could only dream about what a real alien would. Angus wrapped his arm around his petite wife and drew her closer.

"I am claiming your daughter as mine," Borj said as he jerked his head back away from Hannah's again. "She is my bond mate."

"Uh, Borj..." Cosmos began rubbing the back of his neck again. "Uh..."

"Don't you dare, Cosmos Raines. I will castrate you and this alien jerk in your sleep. I'll cut you into little pieces and feed you to the fish. I'll..." Hannah's furious threats were cut short when Borj let out a deep growl and turned Hannah swiftly in his arms. Holding her wrists together behind her back and sliding one leg between hers to prevent her from using her knee again, he crushed his lips against hers in a savage kiss.

Hannah froze in stunned surprise at the heated fury in Borj's kiss. He was laying claim to her in front of her parents, Cosmos, and letting them know he would not take 'no' for an answer. Pulling back briefly, Borj looked into Hannah's dark green eyes fiercely.

"Hannah, please do not fight me," Borj whispered tenderly. *"I knew you were mine from the first time I saw your image. You were beautiful, but it was more than that. There was a look in your eyes that called to me. Please, give me a chance to show you."*

Hannah stood perfectly still as she stared up into Borj's flaming, silver eyes. She could see the sincerity in them. "You don't fight fair," she whispered.

Borj smiled down into Hannah's flushed face. "I will never fight fair where you are concerned."

Tilly and Angus watched the expressions flashing across their oldest daughter's face. For the first time in ten years, Tilly felt a shaft of hope blossoming. She saw the fear and confusion, but she saw something else too. She saw curiosity, hope, and wonder.

"Hannah," Tilly called out softly. "Would you like to introduce your young alien?"

Hannah started at her mother's voice. She closed her eyes briefly with a sinking feeling. Was she the only one blessed with two parents who would think meeting an alien was not only a seemingly everyday occurrence, but totally cool that said alien was showing possessive tendencies over their daughter? Hannah sighed deeply, taking a deep, cleansing breath before she looked back up at Borj.

"Let me go," Hannah said quietly.

Borj shook his head and looked over at Angus, Tilly, and Cosmos with a mischievous grin. "Never," he replied, although he did release one of her wrists so she could turn and look at her parents.

"Hi, mom. Hi, dad. This is Borj. He is from another planet," Hannah said with exaggerated resignation.

CHAPTER SEVEN

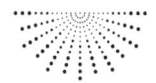

*H*annah's loud groan filled the air as she let her head fall back on the couch. Or, should she say, on Borj's arm on the couch. For the past three hours, her mom and dad had been grilling Borj from everything from how Tink met his brother and how she was doing, to his family, to what did his planet look like, to what base crystals were made of and how they worked. The questions went on and on and on. They would ask, Borj would answer, Cosmos would translate, and Hannah would grit her teeth.

"Argh!" Hannah growled out in frustration finally. "He needs to bring Tink home! I can't believe you two are perfectly okay with your youngest daughter getting knocked up by some over testosterone he-man from another world. What kind of parents are you? Aren't you worried about her?" Hannah growled out trying to get up off the couch – again.

"Of course we are worried, dear. But, from what Cosmos and Borj have said it is because of J'kar that your sister is alive. How can I be upset about that?" Tilly said calmly.

Borj wrapped his arm around Hannah's waist, pulling her closer as she struggled to get up. "Will you knock it off? I am not in the mood to deal with you and them. I need a drink, preferably something with alcohol," Hannah snapped out impatiently.

Her body was doing all sorts of funny things when he touched her and she didn't understand it. She needed to get away from him. She needed time alone to figure out what was going on.

Borj looked with concern at the wild look in Hannah's eyes. He slowly released her, but not before he ran the back of his hand gently down her cheek. Something was wrong. He tried to ask her silently, but she had shut him out.

Tilly watched quietly as Hannah got up and headed for the kitchenette. She was worried about her oldest daughter. Tilly turned her attention back to Borj who was also watching Hannah with worried eyes.

"You must be patient with her. It will take her time to accept you and trust you. She has a very good reason not to trust people," Tilly said softly.

Borj turned his gaze to Tilly. "Why?"

Cosmos cleared his throat before repeating Borj's question. "He wants to know why?"

"It's none of his business," Hannah said quietly from the doorway between the kitchenette and living area. "It is no one's business but mine."

Tilly rose from the chair she was sitting in and walked over to her oldest daughter. Hannah was several inches taller than her mother, but she always felt smaller around her. Tilly wrapped her arms around Hannah and held her. Hannah stood stiffly for a moment before she slowly wrapped her arms around her mom, hugging her back.

"I'm scared, momma," Hannah whispered softly in Tilly's ear. "I don't understand all these strange feelings going on inside me."

Tilly smiled gently and leaned back to brush Hannah's hair back from her face. "I know. What do your feelings tell you when you look at him, sweetheart?" Tilly asked gently.

Hannah looked up and stared into Borj's dark, silver eyes. She could easily drown in them. Hannah focused in on the feelings she felt when she looked into his eyes. She felt… safe, loved, a sense of peace. Borj smiled softly at Hannah. It was as if he knew she was trying to see if she could trust him; not only with her body but with her heart and soul.

"I will always be there for you, my ku lei, always," Borj's voice whispered softly in her mind.

Hannah's eyes darkened with confusion and a small amount of fear. She looked back down at her mom who was waiting patiently for Hannah to work things out in her own mind. Hannah shook her head in denial.

"I don't know," Hannah responded. "I don't understand any of this."

Tilly smiled up encouragingly at Hannah. "Believe in your feelings, Hannah. They have always guided you to safety. They will continue to do so. Now, let's go fix the guys something to eat. Your father has been working on his new book so much he hasn't wanted to eat."

Hannah looked at Cosmos, her dad, and Borj before looking back down at her mom. "I would kill for some pizza. I haven't had one in almost two years. Do you think we could order out?" Hannah begged softly.

"RITA!" Tilly called out.

"Yes, love," RITA replied cheerfully.

"Can you order two pepperoni pizzas with extra cheese, a fresco with spinach and black olives, three dozen wings – mild, and a double order of garlic knots," Tilly called out.

"It will be here in forty-five minutes to an hour. I'll let you know when they pull up," RITA replied.

"Thank you, dear," Tilly called out, pulling Hannah back over to the couch and gently pushing her back into Borj's arms. "Now, tell me again about how Tink met your brother."

Borj settled back against the couch with a sigh. He was beginning to appreciate Cosmos' and Hannah's reluctance at letting Tilly and Angus know about him. He wanted to take Hannah upstairs and wipe the fear and uncertainty out of her eyes. He also needed to return to Baade. The longer he stayed here, the more dangerous it was.

Borj looked at the caution in Angus' eyes and gave a brief nod. He understood Hannah's mother needed reassurance her youngest daughter was safe and happy. He also understood Hannah was not ready to return with him. He wanted to howl out in frustration. He imagined his union would have been much different. More like his brother and Tink's, where Tink seemed unable to keep her hands off of J'kar.

Borj glanced at Hannah out of the corner of his eye. She was trying to sit stiffly so she didn't lean against him, but the soft cushions on the couch made that almost impossible. As he once again told how J'kar and Tink met and about how close they came to losing her, he let his hand gently rub against Hannah's back until he felt her begin to relax and settle closer to him on her own. Yes, her mother was right. It would take time and patience. He would do whatever was necessary for his mate.

Even, Borj thought in despair, *if it killed him.*

∽

Much later, after the pizza and more stories, this time about the adventures of Hannah, Tansy, and Tink growing up, Borj reluctantly settled back down on the couch to sleep. Angus and Tilly left about an hour ago to sleep in their 'motor home'. Borj was fascinated at the idea of someone living in a home that moved around all the time.

This was an interesting world. He liked the different foods and the drink called beer that Cosmos gave him. Borj pulled one of the magazines Cosmos gave him with Hannah's photographs in it out to look through. He rolled over and turned on the small lamp next to the couch. This one was a special edition highlighting Hannah's work from when she was only a child through to last year.

Borj smiled as he looked at the innocent smiling face of Hannah when she was ten. There was a series of photographs ranging from different animals, to people, to landscapes. Each was taken with care and the attention to detail was incredible for one so young. He flipped to the next page. There were several more of Hannah at different ages.

It was when he turned to the next page that he saw a change. She was no longer smiling and her eyes were dark and sad. He turned back to the page before and noted she looked to be about the same age from the one before to the next, but her eyes seemed to have aged a hundred cycles.

Borj growled out in frustration at not being able to read the printed material. Throwing the blanket off of him, he stood up, moving towards the stairs leading up to Hannah. He wanted answers and she made it clear she was the only one who could give them. He took the stairs two at a time on silent feet.

He moved towards the sleeping area. The door was partially closed, but Borj could see just fine, thanks to the lights from the open windows. He walked slowly towards the bed, staring down at Hannah's relaxed face. Sitting carefully on the edge of the bed, he let his gaze move over her face memorizing every detail.

Dark shadows from exhaustion still darkened beneath her eyes even in sleep. Her lips were parted and he could hear the quiet breaths as she breathed in and out slowly. Her hair had come undone from the braid she wore earlier and lay fanned out across the pillows. Borj lifted a hand that wasn't quite steady and gently lifted a strand that lay across her chest.

Hannah could feel she wasn't alone, but she was so tired she didn't want to wake up. Her breath caught in her throat when she felt the warmth of the body as it settled on the mattress next to her. Normally, she would have panicked to have a male so close to her, but instead she felt – protected. She knew immediately who was next to her. She could feel the heat pooling lower between her legs and the restlessness of wanting to be held in his strong arms. Hannah frowned as she felt her body reacting to Borj.

"Tell me what happened to you," Borj asked silently.

"I can't," Hannah whispered back without ever saying a word.

Borj looked into Hannah's dark green eyes that were now staring up at him in a silent plea for understanding. There were the shadows again... the pain and the guilt deep inside begging him to help her find a way to break free from it. As Borj looked deeply into Hannah's eyes, he realized she really couldn't tell him. The anguish, pain, and horror of whatever happened to her were locked so deep inside her for so long she didn't know how to let it out.

Borj let his hand move to cup her cheek gently. *"Then show me,"* he whispered softly in her mind.

Hannah held her breath for a moment before she nodded silently. She instinctively moved her hand up to press it against her cheek so he wouldn't let her go. Borj reached out with his other hand and entwined his fingers with the hand Hannah had lying across her stomach. He squeezed her fingers to let her know he would wait as long as it took for her to trust him. Hannah let out a shaky smile. Never taking her eyes from Borj, she let the memories come. All of them, everything from the shy, shared smiles of a young girl being asked to dance for the first time to the half dead girl who barely made it through the jungle and the nightmares that followed her for years.

Hannah never broke eye contact with Borj. Not even when she relived killing the two men. That was something she never told anyone about, not her parents, not the authorities, not the therapists. The one person who knew what she had done was killed during the rescue attempt and none of the rebels survived to tell.

Hannah's eyes glittered with unshed tears as she stared at Borj waiting for him to condemn her. She should have forced the girl to go with her even if it meant she might be captured. She was a murderer. Even if those men were bad and were doing bad things, she should have found another way to get away without killing them. But the worst was her feelings.

She didn't feel any regret or sorrow for killing the men. She would do it again if she was in the same situation. She felt the same for the girl. She tried to get her to come with her, but she wouldn't. Hannah knew deep down, she would have been raped, killed or both if she had tried to force the girl to go with her. She felt sad for the girl's death, but she didn't regret leaving her. Did that make her a terrible person?

"*Never,*" Borj said tenderly pulling Hannah up into his arms and rocking her back and forth. "*It showed that you are a strong person. You could make the decisions only a leader can. Because of you, others lived. You are a true warrior and I am proud to call you my mate.*"

Hannah didn't say anything. She snuggled further into the Borj's warm body, letting her arms slowly circle his waist and holding him tentatively, like she was afraid he would suddenly disappear. Borj's arms tightened around Hannah and he laid his cheek against her hair.

Now that she let him into her mind fully, he could see other times in her life when she came close to dying. He didn't say anything. He carefully let his mind remain blank as Hannah's memories of other close calls; both from animals and different environments she was photographing to the human predators she encountered flow through him. He absorbed those memories, learning more about Hannah's strength and fierceness.

Borj felt Hannah's body relax against his as exhaustion from the emotional retelling and the stress of not enough sleep finally took hold of her. He continued to hold her tight against his body, even after he knew she was in a deep sleep. Reluctantly, he gently laid her back against the pillows. Moving around the bed, he pulled his jeans off and climbed in next to her. Almost immediately, Hannah rolled over onto her side and burrowed into him. Borj let a small smile curve his lips. She was beginning to trust him whether she wanted to admit it or not.

"Am not," came the soft, teasing whisper in his mind.

Maybe she wasn't as asleep as he thought. Another faint whisper caressed his mind before he knew she really was asleep this time. Borj wrapped his arm around Hannah and closed his eyes. His last thought before exhaustion claimed him was he was already deeply in love with his little warrior.

CHAPTER EIGHT

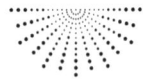

Hannah moaned as another wave of heat flowed through her. The rough palm stroking her breast and pulling on her nipple felt so damn good. Hannah arched her back trying to get closer and froze. Something very long and hard was poking her in the butt… a butt that should have been covered by her boxers which were surprisingly absent. Surprising because she knew darn well she didn't remove them.

"*No, I did. They were in the way,*" Borj whispered quietly in her mind. "*I thought you were never going to wake up.*"

Hannah bit her lip when she felt Borj's warm lips along her shoulder. "You shouldn't be here."

"Why not?" Borj asked curiously as he moved his lips towards Hannah's neck. "I can't think of anywhere I would rather be."

Hannah moved her hand up to still Borj's teasing one on her breast. Rolling over onto her back, she frowned up at Borj. "Listen, you are an alien who will be going back to your world, I am a human who is going to be remaining here. The two don't mix," Hannah tried to explain through a throat that suddenly felt like it was too dry.

Borj let his hand slide down to Hannah's flat stomach. He propped himself up on his elbow so he was gazing down over her. He could feel the fear beginning to build in him and he didn't like it at all. He wanted Hannah to come to him on her own, like Tink did with his brother. He didn't want to have to bite her to make her want him. He wanted... Borj closed his eyes for a moment before opening them again... he wanted Hannah to want to be with him.

"We do mix, Hannah. I plan to take you back to my world with me. I have to return... today. You will come with me. There is no other choice any longer. We have bonded. If you remain here you will die, just as I will die if I return without you," Borj said quietly.

Hannah looked up with a mixture of fear and frustration. She was used to being independent. She could make snap decisions without blinking an eye. She was so totally screwed.

Borj lifted his hand up to brush Hannah's cheek gently. "I do not understand this 'screwed'. I have no wish to hurt you if this is what it means."

Hannah bit her lip. She had two choices: take a chance or tuck tail and run. Since she had never tuck tail and run in her life she decided she might as well take a chance. Reaching up, she pulled Borj down over her. Borj jerked and groaned as he felt Hannah's response. Crushing his lips to hers, he poured all of his love for her into it. This is what it was like, he thought in a daze. This is what it was like to have a connection to someone so deep there was no defining where they separated.

"You are thinking way too much," Hannah groaned as she pulled away slightly. "I thought it was the girl who was supposed to do that."

Borj chuckled. "Something tells me you are not a typical female, even for your world," Borj said as he ran little kisses along Hannah's jaw.

Hannah looked up at Borj for a moment. She stared intently into his flaming silver eyes. "Why do I feel this way about you?" Hannah asked softly.

Borj pressed his swollen cock against Hannah. "I feel the same way about you."

Hannah shook her head slightly from side to side. "No, it is more than that. I feel... safe. I've never felt like that before. Before, if a guy tried to get too close to me I would get all weird," Hannah said puzzled.

"Oh, you still got all weird, dear. You just got over it faster because your body recognized your other half," Tilly Bell said as she stepped into the room.

"Yes, it is amazing what your body knows, isn't it, sweetheart?" Angus said with a slight growl in his voice. "Might I say it was a most enjoyable experience watching your delightful rear-end coming up the stairs."

Hannah gasped, trying to make herself as small as possible under Borj's huge frame. Borj looked over his shoulder at the petite figure of Tilly Bell as she walked over to the side table and set down a small covered tray. Angus moved up behind her handing her the glasses of juice he was carrying. As soon as their hands were free, Angus pulled Tilly into his arms, leaning her over and kissing her hard on the lips.

"You are absolutely beautiful first thing in the morning," Angus whispered softly.

Tilly blushed and grinned up at her husband of almost thirty years. "Oh, you…"

Hannah groaned. "Can you two go get your own room?!"

Angus cleared his throat before gently setting his wife back onto her feet. "Yes, well. We got tired of waiting for you two to come down. From the looks of it, I can understand why now. You should really close the door if you don't want company. Locking it helps too. Anyway, young man, I fully expect for you to do right by my daughter or I will have to take you to task," Angus said sternly pushing his glasses back up on his nose where they had slipped down.

Borj looked Angus up and down through half-closed eyes trying not to show his amusement at the man's stern threat. He easily outweighed Hannah's father by a hundred pounds or more and was almost a foot taller. Not to mention, Borj was built like all Prime males, very muscular, where Angus was obviously not.

"Don't under-estimate them. It's not my dad you have to worry about, it's my mom. She could kick your ass while drinking a cup of coffee," Hannah warned.

Borj looked at the sweet looking little woman next to Angus and shook his head. *"I could crush her with one fist."*

"Yeah, like you did me?" Hannah asked with a raised eyebrow.

Borj flushed as he remembered how quickly Hannah knocked him on his ass. He was just about to say something when Tilly sat down on the bed next to them. Borj tightened his arms around Hannah, who tried to the hide the impossible fact that she was naked with Borj still on top of her.

"Your forehead is looking much better. Hannah, you did a good job. I saw the dents in Tink's frying pan. How many times did you hit him?" Tilly said totally ignoring both her oldest daughter's discomfort and Borj's as she brushed his hair back from his forehead to peer at the discolored bruise.

"Twice," Hannah groaned. "Mom. Dad. This is a little embarrassing. Do you think you can leave so we can get up?"

Tilly peeked down at Hannah with a wide grin. "Oh, I'd say he was already up," she giggled.

"Yes, it would seem Borj was having a bit of a *hard* time with our little girl." Hannah's face flamed as her father joined in on the joke. "Come, dear. I think we have our answer. We have some packing to do if we are going to be going with them," Angus said reaching for his giggling wife.

Hannah let out a deep breath and let her head fall back on the bed with a loud groan. "Why? What did I ever do to deserve such weird parents? Maybe I was adopted or found as a baby. I keep hoping," Hannah muttered humorously.

Borj rolled over. There was nothing like having his mate's parents in the room to douse the fire of passion. Looking over at Hannah, who was staring up at the ceiling with a small grin on her face, he thought it might not be doused all the way when his cock jerked again.

Hannah turned and looked at Borj. "Do you have any idea of what you are getting not only yourself into but your planet? This is just a taste of my parents; the very teeny, tiny tip of the iceberg," she said with a small frown.

Borj pulled Hannah over on top of him enjoying her gasp of surprise. He looked down at her breasts, watching as the tips hardened before his eyes. The responsiveness of her to him pulled at his own body.

He would face a hundred Tilly and Angus Bell's if it meant having Hannah, Borj thought as his eyes grew heavy with need again.

"I hope so," Hannah said, responding to his quietly muttered vow. "I really hope so."

~

An hour later, Hannah was standing downstairs in Cosmos' living quarters glaring at her grinning parents. They were worse than a couple of high school teenagers going on a field trip! Her mom was actually bouncing with excitement while her dad just looked with amusement at Hannah.

"No, you two are not going!" Hannah said with a fierce look at her mother. "We don't know what is there. It could be dangerous. We're talking about an alien world filled with god-knows-what, for crying out loud!" Hannah threw an apologetic look at Borj. "No insult intended."

Borj bowed his head in acknowledgement of Hannah's frustration. *"I will make you apologize later… in bed,"* he told her before adding, *"in my living quarters with the doors barricaded against all intruders, including your parents."*

Hannah flushed. Borj would have happily continued what they started this morning, but Hannah couldn't get past the nervousness that her parents would barge in again. Not to mention, she almost made love in her little sister's bed. That just wasn't right, even if Tink might not be using it anymore.

"Oh course we are going. We are all packed. Your father can write there and I want to see what type of power structures they have in place. We'll spend time with Tink and her new hubby and help her with the babies. Oh, me… grandchildren. I can't wait for you and Borj to have some. I am going to have so much fun spoiling them," Tilly continued on and on as if Hannah never said anything.

Hannah threw her arms up in the air. *THIS is why I don't come home that often,* she thought in frustration. At least with the animals it didn't matter if they didn't listen to her. Hannah growled at Cosmos as he bit back a chuckle.

"I tried, but they wouldn't listen to me either," Cosmos said in humor. "Your dad already parked the RV in the loading bay. He had their luggage in the lab, thanks to RITA letting him in, as well."

"I plead the fifth, dear," RITA called out. "I was just following orders."

"Hannah, Tink needs us," Angus said quietly, looking at his oldest daughter. He didn't add he felt like she could use the moral support too. "Please let your mom and I go."

"Oh, daddy," Hannah whispered. She never could turn her dad down. "Do you two promise to try to be good? At least a little? No hanky-panky in the hallways? No giving advice on sex?"

Tilly looked at Borj who quickly shook his head. "Oh, I won't say a word unless they ask me. I swear," Tilly said with a pleased smile.

"Okay," Hannah said doubtfully. Turning around to Borj, she bit her bottom lip. "You are totally screwing up my life. You better be worth it," she said, poking her finger into his chest.

∽

Hannah packed her backpack again with her usual traveling items. A couple of cargo pants, some tank tops, two button up shirts to wear as covers, a hoodie, and extra underwear and socks. She also had her small bag of toiletries and her camera bags. Glancing around, she didn't see anything she missed. Slinging the backpack onto her shoulder, she bit back the wave of panic threatening her. This was so far out of her comfort zone she didn't even know where to begin.

"I will be there for you. You will love my world," Borj brushed against her mind.

"I won't be locked up," Hannah whispered back fiercely. *"I need space. I need to be outside. I need freedom."*

"I would never lock you up. You are like the delicate Ta'caras. I will protect you, but not cage you, ku lei," Borj assured her softly.

Hannah nodded, even though she knew Borj couldn't see. Straightening her shoulders, she reminded herself she was in control. This was her choice. She wanted to see where these strange and confusing feelings would take her.

She bit back a smile when she remembered her wish just a few weeks ago. She wished to find a warrior who was strong enough and brave enough and honest enough for her to trust. Well, she found him or he found her depending on whose perspective you were looking at. What was funny was her doubt there was a man on Earth who could make her feel this way. Turns out, there wasn't a human man on Earth, but an alien one.

⁓

After many promises to Cosmos that additional visits were more than likely and extracting a solemn promise not to mention any of this to Tansy, Borj opened the portal. Tilly's enthusiastic cry of wonder and Angus' chuckle of amazement were lost on Hannah as more waves of doubt and uncertainty flooded her. She could not believe she was doing this. A cold sweat broke out over her body as she drew back. She knew once she made the final step there would be no going back. She would be committing herself to both a new world and to Borj.

Borj looked back and held his hand out for Hannah. He smiled gently, as if understanding her fear. It was the look in his eyes that gave Hannah the courage to know she was doing the right thing. Placing her trembling palm in Borj's, she threaded her fingers through his and walked through the shimmering doorway after her parents.

"Oh, Angus! Look at these handsome devils. They are almost as cute as you," Tilly was saying as she walked around the two guards stationed inside the room set up with the portal device.

⁓

Borj stood before his father and the council with a weary frown. The moment they returned the guards informed him he was to meet with the council. Borj insisted on escorting Tilly and Angus to the guest living quarters. He wanted to escort Hannah to his but she insisted on staying with her parents until they saw Tink and made sure she was alright.

Borj sent a message to J'kar that Tink's parents and sister were waiting for her. J'kar's growl let him know he must have interrupted him at a bad time. He brushed a hard kiss across Hannah's lips before he left. He wanted her to know he would be returning for her and there would be no more delays in his claiming of her. Already he could feel the desperate edge building inside him. He could not, would not, be denied any longer.

"You returned with more family members than we requested," one of the council members stated looking down at Borj with a frown.

"It was unavoidable. The female and her parents were both there. I have claimed the female called Hannah as my bond mate," Borj said fiercely.

"Your bond mate?" another council member said in stun surprise. "You have proof of this?"

Borj gave a sharp nod of his head and held up his left palm for all the council members to see. "The moment we touched, the mating marks appeared. She is mine."

Several of the council members rose partially out of their chairs to see the mark better. Others whispered back and forth between themselves. Teriff looked on impatiently at the other members tapping his fingers on the curved table.

"He has a bond mate. The female had no choice but to be brought back with him. The council stated the mother was to be brought, she was. The fact her mate was brought as well is to be expected. Perhaps these humans need to have their mates to survive like the Prime. He followed his orders and returned. I call this meeting to an end," Teriff said loudly, bringing his fist down so hard on the curved table it vibrated loudly throughout the council chambers.

"But, what if these humans told others about the portal? What security measures are in place?" one council member voiced in an irritated tone.

"What about other females? Our males need a chance to acquire a bond mate. If word gets out that only the royal family has access there could be trouble," another voiced loudly.

One of the older council members voiced his concern. "What of the other clans? Once they find out we have access to a world where bond mates are possible they will attack."

"How would they find out?" another asked.

"The human male," a tall, muscular council member said just loud enough for Borj to hear over the other councilmen's loud voices.

Borj's head jerked around to Te'mar. He was the newest member of the council. Te'mar inherited the position after his father was injured in an accident. His father decided afterwards to retire. Te'mar was their former Captain of the Guard and was very familiar with the other clans that made up the Prime world, especially the elusive Eastern Mountain clan. Te'mar looked grim as he stared at Borj. He nodded once briefly to let Borj know he had information he wasn't ready to tell the others. Borj returned his stare. Something was up and he feared it meant danger to the human females.

CHAPTER NINE

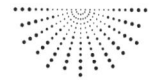

After another round of heated arguments, questions, possible solutions and veiled threats from Teriff to beat the lot of them if they didn't finish up, the council finally adjourned for the day. Borj waited outside the council chamber doors for Te'mar. As much as he wanted to get back to Hannah, he knew her safety had to come first. He needed to know what Te'mar knew.

Teriff looked at Borj as he came through the doors. He had a frown on his face. Teriff nodded stiffly to several of the other council members as they left. Borj tried not to show the amusement he felt at the obvious impatience on his father's face.

"Bunch of old men," Teriff grumbled under his breath as two more council members slowly moved by them. "They have been on the council since before I was born. We need some more young blood like Te'mar."

Borj looked at his father in surprise. This was the first time he heard him comment on the age of some of the other council members. One or more must have made him mad.

"What have they done now?" Borj asked with a straight face.

"As your brother's mate says 'they need to get laid'," Teriff responded. "They want to have longer sessions to figure out what to do with this human male who killed the guards and escaped. We have some of our best trackers on the task. I say kill him and be done with it. It is only a matter of time before he is found. What would additional meetings to discuss it do?" Teriff growled out as he adjusted the front of his pants.

Borj was about to comment when Te'mar came out of the chamber. He looked grimly at both Borj and Teriff. He didn't slow down as he moved towards his office further down the corridor. Borj and Teriff raised an eyebrow before following. Once inside, Te'mar moved to a small cabinet and poured an amber liquid into a small glass. He handed one to Teriff before pouring two more. He handed one to Borj before picking up the last for himself. He turned toward the long, narrow set of windows and took a deep gulp of his drink before turning around.

"The Eastern Mountain Clan has knowledge of the females but not the portal. The human male showed them the holovid of J'kar's mate," Te'mar said darkly.

"Where is the human male now?" Borj asked quietly, absorbing the information and calculating the possible outcomes. None of them seemed good.

"He has requested protection from the Eastern Mountain Clan in return for giving them information about human females. Fortunately, there was nothing about the portal and he was unconscious when he was brought aboard the *Prime Destiny*," Te'mar responded.

"Why didn't they just kill him?" Teriff growled out. "Who gave you this information?"

Te'mar looked coldly at Teriff. It was true Teriff was his commanding officer and leader of their world, but some things were best left unknown. His promise long ago held his lips tight. There were some things even he was not at liberty to share. He could answer the first question, though.

"They almost did. It was only when they were about to kill him that the holovid was played. They demanded he tell them of the female. He made a deal with them to show them where to find the females and give them more information on them in exchange for protection. You should know as well as I do how desperate the men of our world are getting. I have been to over sixteen mating ceremonies myself and never found my bond mate," Te'mar looked at Borj. "Now that you have found yours, would you give her up?" he asked quietly.

"Never!" Borj said fiercely, slamming his glass down before he broke it. "Never," he said more calmly. "I have not totally claimed her yet, but our bond is already strong. I can hear her thoughts and share her feelings. It is like I am finally complete," Borj looked at Te'mar then at his father. "I don't feel the emptiness and desperate ache anymore and I have not even claimed her physically yet," he said quietly.

"Borj, are you alright?" Hannah's soft voice brushed against his mind.

"Yes," Borj whispered back. *"I will be with you soon."*

Just as quickly, she was gone, but not all the way. He could still feel the connection between them. It must have shown briefly on his face because Te'mar finished his drink and slammed his own glass down on his desk.

"This is what I mean. The men are desperate for a mate. The population of females is at a critical level. The few females that are old enough have already bonded with a male except for a small number like your daughter, Terra. Soon, the males will not care if she is their bond mate or not. One of them will just claim her," Te'mar said darkly.

Teriff's face flushed a deep red and Borj felt his own temper rise at the silent threat to their family. "Never! I will kill any male who tries to claim Terra without being her bond mate," Teriff growled out dangerously.

Te'mar shook his head. "Your best bet would be to send her away someplace safe. Even the palace walls are no longer a safe place for an unclaimed female of age."

∽

Borj stood in the doorway watching as Hannah laughed at something Tink was saying. Tilly Bell was sitting on the couch with her 'husband's' arm around her shoulder sipping on a drink. His brother, J'kar, had a dark scowl on his face as he tried to catch Tink, who was moving around rapidly while retelling how she met J'kar in an animated voice.

His mother was seated in one of the other chairs. He looked around, but did not see his sister, Terra. Hannah looked up and smiled softly at Borj.

"How was your meeting?" Hannah asked curiously. "Your mom said she wasn't expecting anyone else except my mom."

"Yes, well…" Borj said with a sheepish grin. "After I explained that you were there and I had no choice but to bring you, they understood."

J'kar looked at Borj in amusement as he finally caught Tink as she twirled by him and pulled her onto his lap. "Yes. It had nothing to do with the image you were carrying or the fact you refused to obey a direct order," J'kar chuckled out.

Borj's face flushed as he looked at Hannah's parents and his mother. "I knew she was my bond mate the moment I saw her. I just didn't expect our first meeting to be so painful an experience," he said, touching the fading bruise on his forehead.

Hannah just grinned with a non-sympathetic look on her face. "That'll teach you to sneak around in the dark."

Tilly laughed with delight. "You tell him, Hannah. Borj, you should see the frying pan. It is in much worse shape than your head."

"You clobbered him with a frying pan? Man, that must have hurt!" Tink said in awe.

"Yes, but not as much as the knee did," Hannah added without thinking.

"The knee?" J'kar asked with a frown.

Tink, Tilly, and Hannah all burst out laughing as Angus gave Borj a sympathetic glance. "Hannah has very good reflexes and her mother made sure all the girls learned basic self-defense," Angus said with a slightly apologetic sigh.

Borj's hand moved to rub the front of his pants in remembrance. "Yes, so I discovered the hard way." There was another burst of laughter from the women at Borj's response.

"What of the meeting, Borj?" his mother, Tresa, asked quietly as the laughter settled down.

Borj sighed heavily as he moved to pull Hannah up out of the chair she was sitting in long enough to sit before pulling her onto his lap.

Hannah started to move, but Borj wrapped his arm determinedly around her waist holding her to him. He was holding onto his patience by a thread. He knew she would not appreciate him throwing her over his shoulder, but if he didn't claim her soon that was exactly what was going to happen.

"Feeling a little frustrated and impatient, are we?" Hannah teased silently wiggling her ass just enough to feel something harden underneath it.

Hannah fought to keep the blush from her face as she felt Borj's cock swelling to an incredible size under her. *"I will show you how impatient I am soon, ku lei,"* Borj replied with a dark promise.

Hannah froze as she absorbed what was happening. She was actually teasing Borj! This was so new to her, she wasn't sure what to think or feel. Analyzing it, she decided she liked it.

She liked the sense of power it gave her to know Borj reacted that way to her, but she also liked the feeling coursing through her. There was that excited adrenaline rush she got during a dangerous photo shoot or when she knew everything was just right. Her sixth sense was telling her that this was right.

Hannah looked at her mom and noticed she was watching her with a soft, understanding smile lighting her eyes. She looked to her dad and he gave her a wink and a small nod. Hannah's lips curved as she blushed and inclined her head shyly.

"Borj?" Tresa asked again breaking into his thoughts. "The council?"

"Everything went as expected. Once I proved my claim on Hannah they understood I had no choice but to return with her. I also explained it would be unfair to expect their mother to be forcibly removed from her mate since we knew what happens when we are separated from our own," Borj said quietly. He paused for a moment looking at J'kar before continuing. "There was also concern about the human male that was brought back. It appears he is under the protection of the Eastern Mountain Clan. He made promises of telling them of the human females," Borj said darkly.

J'kar sat forward, tightening his grip around Tink. "How did you learn this? I have not received a report from Lan yet," J'kar responded harshly.

"Te'mar. He would not say what his source was but I believe him. He said Bachman was about to be terminated when the holovid was discovered. Once played, he used it as a bargaining tool...his life for more information on human females. Fortunately, there was nothing about the portal on it and he was unconscious when he was taken. Te'mar fears they will try to take the females and use them to find out how they came here and where their planet is," Borj informed all of them.

"Oh, dear. That could be a problem," Tilly said, leaning back against Angus. "How secure are the portal devices and the room? Cosmos needs to be aware as well, so he can set up additional security on his end."

"I'm sure they are already working on that, sweetheart," Angus assured his wife. He turned to look at J'kar. "I am concerned with the safety of my wife and daughters here, though. I won't have anything happen to them," Angus said forcefully.

"I have already posted additional guards throughout the palace," J'kar assured Angus.

"Nevertheless, I would like to see what arrangements have been set in place. While I may not be a warrior such as yourselves, I am a writer. As a writer, I can often see things other people tend to miss or overlook. You would be surprised at how many countries I have been to and found ways around their security systems by doing some simple research and observations," Angus said firmly letting both men know he would not stand passively by if there was a possibility of his family being in danger.

Borj bowed his head in acknowledgement. "You have a right to know as the male of your family. I will have Lan meet with you and your beautiful mate to review our security measures," Borj said quietly looking to J'kar who also nodded in agreement.

Tilly sniffed indignantly at the mention of Angus being the 'male' of the family but bit her tongue. It would appear there were quite a few things these aliens needed to learn besides how to let a female have fun during sex. Tilly relaxed back as she felt Angus gently squeeze her shoulder in understanding. He knew her so well.

"Was there anything else?" J'kar asked as he gently rubbed Tink's still flat belly.

"Te'mar also mentioned concern about Terra," Borj continued, hesitantly looking at his mother.

J'kar frowned. "What about Terra?" he growled out lowly.

Tink patted her hands over his. "Down boy, you're squeezing."

J'kar muttered a silent apology and kissed the back of Tink's neck, enjoying the shiver that ran through his mate at the touch of his lips. As soon as he found out what threat there was to Terra he was taking his mate back to their living quarters. He grimaced when he felt Tink's elbow in his ribs. He must have been thinking loudly again.

"You were. I guess I'll just have to tie you up and have my wicked way with you. Maybe I can..." J'kar groaned as the vivid pictures Tink began thinking made him swell with need.

Tilly glanced at the pained expression on J'kar's face in fascination. "Is she talking dirty to you, sweetheart? You look like Angus after we've been..." Tilly's words died as Angus swung her around to silence her with his lips.

Hannah groaned while Tink giggled. "Aw, mom! This is visual information your children really don't need to know," Hannah said, closing her eyes as her mom started running her hands over her dad. "Borj, just tell J'kar what you were going to say so we can leave these two alone. They have a new place to initiate."

Tink laughed out loud. "Yeah, they have a whole new planet, you mean."

Borj cleared his throat as he watched with growing hunger as Angus reluctantly released his wife. Both of them were breathing a little heavy and had a glazed look on their face. Angus pushed his glasses back into place before nodding for Borj to continue.

"Te'mar is afraid some of the men are getting desperate at not being able to find their bond mate. There are a few females who are of age and still unclaimed. Terra is one of them. He fears the men will no longer wait to see if a bond mate can be found for these females but take them against their will. He wonders if even the palace is safe enough to protect her. Others have sent their unclaimed females to the Island of Maree until the next mating ceremony. He suggested it might be better to send Terra away as well," Borj explained in a reserved voice.

J'kar frowned while Tresa gasped. "But, it is so far. How would she be safer away from her family? She would hate it. It is like a prison. You know she will refuse. There is nothing for her to do there. Her research, her love of…" Tresa's voice faded at the resigned look on both of her sons' faces.

"Father has already agreed to send her," Borj said quietly hating the pain he saw come across his mother's face.

Angus cleared his throat before speaking. "I know this is none of my business, but are you sure that is a wise decision? I mean, sending all the 'unclaimed' females to this place? It seems to be the perfect set up for disaster. You have all your eggs in one basket. No matter how secure it may appear, no place is completely invincible. You've just placed all the females in an easier place to be taken in a large number," Angus said frowning as different scenarios ran through his head.

J'kar looked at Angus for a moment. "What would you suggest then to protect her?"

"I know!" Tink said excitedly. "I know!"

"What, sweetheart?" Tilly asked curiously.

"Send her to Cosmos! Then you know no one can get her! Between Cosmos and RITA they can make sure no one comes through and he will protect her. He also has the lab there. She loves to tinker as much as he does," Tink said excitedly.

"She could have your old room," Hannah said with a growing smile. "He would do everything he could to protect her."

"Never! Look what happened to you on your world," J'kar growled out fiercely.

"And to you," Borj said quietly but just as fiercely.

"Nonsense," Tilly responded calmly. "Those were both very isolated occurrences. Plus, if Cosmos knows Terra is under his protection he will be very diligent to ensure her safety."

"She's right. I would trust Cosmos with all three of my daughters and have," Angus added.

"But, she would be alone with the male," J'kar growled out protectively.

Tink twisted in J'kar's lap and grabbed both sides of his face, forcing him to look her in the eye. "So was I, for several years. He is the perfect gentleman," Tink growled out in a voice that warned J'kar he was walking on thin ice if he was thinking of insulting Cosmos.

Borj rubbed his chin before responding. "I have met the male and he did seem very protective of Hannah and Tink. Terra would be much happier there than on Maree. The only problem would be getting father's agreement to sending her."

Tresa smiled suddenly. "Oh, I don't think that will be much of a problem. I have gotten very good at getting his agreement. I think with Tilly's help, I can come up with some very creative ways to get him to change his mind," Tresa said with a mischievous smile curving her delicate lips.

Tilly's eyes brightened. "I have just the thing. I brought all of Cosmos' magazines he had hidden. I'm sure we can get some wonderful ideas from them."

Hannah groaned while Tink's mouth formed a silent 'oh'. Angus chuckled. "Perhaps, we can help test some of those ideas ourselves," he growled out softly against his wife's ear.

CHAPTER TEN

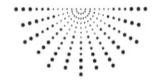

Borj walked slowly through the corridors with Hannah tucked securely at his side. It took every ounce of his considerable self-restraint not to just pick her up and run with her to his living quarters. He couldn't hear her fears as she was blocking him from her mind, but he could feel the slight tremble in her fingers which were laced through his.

"Open your mind to mine. Let me be one with you," Borj requested gently.

Hannah stumbled a little over her own feet and gripped Borj's hand tightly. "I'm afraid to," she whispered.

Borj stopped and backed Hannah into one of the many side alcoves along the corridor. "Why are you afraid?" Borj asked gently.

Hannah looked up at Borj. He gently brushed a strand of her hair that had come undone from her braid back behind her ear. Borj stared down into Hannah's eyes and saw the uncertainty in them. Cupping her face with one hand, he brushed his lips across hers. He groaned softly when he felt her shy response. The soft, tentative touch almost tore his delicate thread on sanity apart. He leaned his forehead against hers and breathed deeply, trying to hold his desires back.

"Why?" Borj asked. "Why are you afraid?"

Hannah pulled back far enough to look into Borj's eyes. "What if I can't? I tried before... to be with a man that way... but I couldn't do it. I had a panic attack," Hannah gave a self-deprecating laughed. "Give me lions, warlords, and the most hostile environment on Earth and I'm as calm as they come. Give me a hot male and sex and I'm a basket case."

Borj growled low at the thought of another male touching Hannah the way he wanted to. Dark flames appeared in his eyes as jealousy swirled deep inside his gut. She was his. Borj's head jerked up when he felt Hannah's hands on his face between her palms.

"I said tried. Never got past first base. He had to stop kissing me to get a paper bag. Do you have any idea what a turnoff that was? It was so bad he called my mom to come get me. He was terrified I was going to die on him! Trust me when I say he never called to ask me out again," Hannah said as she saw the flames flickering in his eyes.

Boy, who would have thought a guy being a little jealous could be such a turn on. Hannah was beginning to think she had a lot more of her parents and Tink in her than she thought! Between the growl and the flames all she could think about now was not how nervous she was but how much she wanted to see if she could make him make other noises.

"Maybe I've been out with the wild things a little too long," Hannah murmured as she pressed her lips against Borj's in a desperate kiss.

Borj wrapped his arms tightly around Hannah. Her kiss was filled with the same desperate need he was feeling. Unwilling to give her a chance to regret her decision, he swept her up into his arms. Breaking the kiss, he turned quickly moving toward his living quarters in determination. She would be his. He nodded to the two guards who watched him approach in awe. Both of the guards were fascinated by the female who was pressing desperate kisses into Borj's neck. One quickly opened the door for Borj as he came closer. Both guards let their gaze turn to Hannah's flushed face only turning away when Borj growled out a warning.

Borj caught the door with his foot slamming it shut. Holding Hannah tightly against him, Borj ordered the door to seal and not open unless he gave the command. He would not take the chance of them being interrupted this time.

"No problem, honey. I've set the locks and only you or Hannah can get me to undo them. I won't even let Tilly or Tink in," RITA's voice came on over the system.

Hannah jerked her lips away from Borj's neck where she was running her tongue in little swirls along his pulse. "RITA?" Hannah choked out in a combination of amazement and horror.

"You have RITA here too?!" Hannah asked Borj.

Borj gritted his teeth and replied. "It would appear she has managed to get off the *Prime Destiny* and taken over our programming in the palace."

"Oh, there's nothing to worry about. Brock and Lan asked me to take a look at the programming you have here. Well, actually they only wanted me to look at the portal programming, but it was just too much of a temptation not to look at some of the other and one thing led to another. Did you know…" RITA was saying.

Hannah groaned and buried her face against Borj's neck. "I warned you. Now, you have Tink, my parents, and RITA. Your world will never be the same. Just don't let Cosmos and Tansy in. I'm not sure it could handle all of them together in one place," Hannah whispered.

"I heard that, Hannah May Bell! You know, I think I've changed my mind. Borj, dear, only you can let Hannah out of this room. I think it only right to help make sure she doesn't escape. You know her parents have been trying to set her up with some of the nicest boys but she just wasn't interested. Now that I've seen you, I can understand why. You are totally hot. She doesn't stand a chance," RITA continued.

"RITA!" Borj growled out as he continued moving toward his sleeping quarters.

"Yes, dear?" RITA asked.

"Leave us. I want privacy," Borj commanded determinedly as he set Hannah down next to the bed.

"Oh, of course. Sorry, sweetheart. I'll pop in later to see if you need anything," RITA said cheerfully.

Hannah closed her eyes. "She's going to tell my mom I'm finally going to get laid. I just know it," Hannah hissed out softly in annoyance.

Borj gripped the front of Hannah's shirt and tore it off her. Hannah's eyes popped open as she heard the material tearing. Her hands started to rise up to cover her breasts, but Borj's snarl of warning stilled them.

The combination of his aggressiveness and the flames burning in his eyes was enough to send moist heat pooling between Hannah's legs. Her eyes widened in surprise before closing halfway as she watched Borj sink to his knees in front of her. She watched as he pulled the button loose on her cargo pants and lowered the zipper. He brushed a kiss across her stomach and along her hip as he pulled them down her legs.

"You are mine, Hannah. Forever," Borj's heated breath whispered against her skin.

A shiver raced through Hannah's body. This time it had nothing to do with fear and everything to do with wanting the man in front of her. He pulled first one of her boots off then the other. Hannah placed one hand on Borj's shoulder to steady herself as he removed them. She could feel the tense muscles under her hand as he fought to control his own desires. She couldn't resist letting her other hand run through his short hair.

"You make me feel so much," Hannah whispered, opening her mind so he could see and feel what she was feeling. "You make feel beautiful, loved… safe. I never thought I would ever feel safe again."

Borj looked up into Hannah's shimmering eyes and knew at that moment he would die a thousand deaths before he let her ever be harmed again. He finished pulling her pants off, leaving her standing in nothing more than her lacy bra and panties. He rose slowly letting his hands travel up her smooth thighs to her waist. He never took his eyes from hers, holding her as captive as she was him. His hands trembled with a combination of overwhelming feelings and need as he drew her long, willowy length against his harder one.

"I claim you as my bond mate, Hannah, as my wife for all time. The council is aware of our bond and has approved our union," Borj said as he brushed a tender kiss along Hannah's jaw. "You are so precious to me. I never thought to find my bond mate. I had resigned myself to living a solitary life, but you… you have filled my life and my soul."

Hannah couldn't reply over the lump in her throat. She leaned forward, wrapping her arms around Borj's neck and pulling him down to her in a passionate kiss filled with all her love and longing. There was no doubt in her mind that she loved him. How could she not when he touched a part of her no one else ever had.

Borj gently lowered Hannah down on the bed. He fought for a moment with the clasp on her bra before snapping it impatiently in frustration when he couldn't get it undone fast enough. Hannah giggled when he pulled away far enough to frown down at her.

"You are not allowed to wear those things any more. How the *hockta balmas* can a male get to a female with one of those on?" Borj muttered darkly as he tossed the offending bra away.

"It has a clasp in the back. You undo them. They help give a girl lift and support," Hannah murmured against Borj's lips with a small chuckle. "I need you Borj," Hannah whispered softly.

Borj's eyes flared at the words a Prime male never thought to hear openly from a female. He could feel his canines begin to extend. He saw Hannah's eyes widen as she saw his teeth growing longer as his need to claim her exploded through him. Hannah let her hand move up to touch one gently with the tip of her finger. Her eyes darted back and forth between his mouth and his eyes. He waited for the fear. Even Prime females sometimes expressed fear at the show of a male's desire. Instead, he saw curiosity and wonder.

"Does it hurt?" Hannah breathed out as her eyes darted to his quickly before returning to his mouth. "Why?"

Borj pressed his swollen groin against Hannah's hot mound. "Normally a Prime male has to bite a female to get her ready to accept him. It was not always so. According to the archives, a male would bite a female only when the bonded couple wished to mate. Our bite contains a chemical that prepares a female's womb for our seed. The chemical also increases the enjoyment of the coupling between the male and the female," Borj said, rocking his hips back and forth with a groan.

He did not add that his teeth became very sensitive as they

extended. This increased his enjoyment as well. Hannah's gentle touch was arousing him to impossible levels. His cock rebelled against the constraint of his pants. He thought to wait to remove his clothing wanting to take his time, but he was not going to make it. All rational thought disappeared when Hannah reached up and ran her tongue along one of the extended canines.

"Oh, gods!" Borj choked out.

He pulled away from Hannah forcibly. Standing, he shed his clothing uncaring if he tore the front of his pants or his shirt. His eyes were blazing silver flames as he stood for just a moment over Hannah before he growled out a fierce snarl of passion.

Hannah backed up on the bed as Borj's face darkened with desire. He came down on the bed, grabbing Hannah's legs and pulling them apart as he pulled her closer to him. He ignored her surprised cry. He could smell her aroused scent and it inflamed him even further. Borj let one of his hands move up to rip Hannah's panties away from her moist mound and buried his face against her.

"Oh!" Hannah's breath released on an outward gasp as the sensations overwhelmed her. She spread her legs even further wanting more. "Oh, Borj!"

Hannah's fingers tightened in Borj's short hair as she threw her head back as waves of heat broke over her. Her breath caught in her throat as Borj used his mouth and tongue on her in ways she only heard or read about. Hannah's loud moan filled the room as Borj pushed two thick fingers inside her hot channel.

A sharp tug on her clit combined with his fingers moving inside her was too much for her already excited body. Her body exploded as her orgasm shook her delicious wave after delicious wave. Borj refused to release his grip on her thighs as he continued to drink her essence groaning as it ignited his blood.

Breaking away from Hannah, he moved slowly up her body. He let his canines scrape along her skin gently. He could feel the chemical at the hollowed tips seeping out. He wanted to take Hannah without biting her first, but knew it would be impossible because of his own arousal. He could not believe how explosive she reacted in his arms without having to bite her. Never had he heard of this before his brother's mate. The power of the feelings coursing through him made his heart beat fast with excitement and joy.

Borj pulled his body over Hannah, caging her within his arms. He stared down into her dazed eyes, the look in them firing his already heated blood. He settled his heavy cock between her legs still spread wide from his tonguing of her clit. He watched her eyes dilate as the hot tip of his cock pressed against her swollen folds demanding entrance. Her breathing increased to almost a pant as she arched her back in an attempt to get closer.

"Please!" Hannah begged as her breathing came faster. "I need you so badly, I hurt. Love me, Borj. Claim me and never let me go."

Borj's restraint dissolved at Hannah's breathless plea. With a surge, he took her in one thrust breaking through the barrier and settling deeply into her womb at the same time as he sunk his teeth into the curve where her shoulder and neck met. Hannah's body convulsed under his at the intense pleasure/pain of his thrust and bite followed by the release of the chemical into her blood stream that coursed through her body.

Borj held still as he let Hannah's body adjust to his. The muscles in his neck stood out as he forced his body to obey him. He continued to let the chemical in his canines release as the sweet taste of Hannah's blood seeped around the wound into his mouth. He moaned as his cock jerked deep inside Hannah against his will. The feel and taste of her was so good, so intense he felt like he was dying.

Hannah felt the pain, but it was insignificant compared to the other feelings burning through her. She could feel the fire of his bite as the chemical moved rapidly through her, singeing her as the heat built. Her body was trapped under Borj's; held tight in the cage of his arms, held still by his grip on her shoulder, and impaled by his throbbing cock.

She should have felt intense fear. Instead, she felt a need, a want that screamed for fulfillment. Hannah moved her hips in a slightly circular motion to get him to understand she needed him to move. She wanted to feel everything he had to give to her. Scraping her nails down his back to grab his ass, she pulled her legs up far enough to wrap them around the back of his thighs.

"Fuck me, Borj," Hannah moaned. "Move for me. Take me hard. I want to feel what it's like when you lose control. Give me everything, my love. Love me," Hannah breathed as she moved her hips and brushed her breasts against his chest.

"Gods, Hannah. You do not know what you ask," Borj muttered as he gently licked at the mark he left on her delicate skin. "I could hurt you."

"Never," Hannah said with a brilliant smile as she realized it was true. She knew deep down he could never hurt her.

Borj pulled partially out of her and slammed back in letting her feel the full length of his cock. Both of them groaned as the heated friction pulled at them as he moved. Borj opened his mind to Hannah letting her see and feel the images and feeling coursing through him.

He knew the moment she saw his desire for her. He held nothing back. Not the ways he wanted to claim her, his love and need for not only her body but her companionship, nothing. He let his loneliness and years of pushing his own wants and needs aside for his people show. He shared his deepest longing... his secret yearning for someone to share his life with and to watch her grow round with his children.

"Never again," Hannah said, understanding his feelings which mirrored her own. "You'll never be alone again, I promise."

Borj stared into Hannah's eyes as he began moving faster and harder. He never took his eyes off hers even as he felt the tightening in his balls as his orgasm built. Her hot channel fought to hold him to her, causing a delicious friction all along his cock. He fought his own need as long as he could before it exploded out of him in fiery streams of hot seed deep inside Hannah's womb. His hoarse cry of release was pulled from the very depths of his soul as he found the plane of peace only the claiming of his bond mate could bring deep inside him.

Hannah gasped as she felt the heated release deep inside her and Borj's hard shaft jerking as his release came hot and heavy inside her. Her own body reacted to his, clamping down like a vicious fist around his cock, refusing to let him pull out until she was ready. Hannah didn't even realize her fingernails were drawing blood as she gripped Borj's arms as she came again. Her cries burst from her lips as if she was shattering into a million pieces.

Borj dropped down until his head rested in the curve of Hannah's shoulder, breathing deeply in an attempt to calm his racing pulse. Never, never in all his long years had he ever felt anything so intense and fulfilling. He could feel Hannah's own heart beating as one with his own.

"We are one, *ku lei*. We belong forever to each other," Borj said possessively.

"I can handle forever if it is anything like this. I can't believe I was so afraid to try this before! I feel like every bone in my body has melted into a liquid pool on the bed," Hannah mused in sated wonder.

Borj growled out at the image of Hannah letting another man claim her. He felt his cock jerk in answer to his possessiveness. He wanted to fill her with his essence so there was no mistake as to who she belonged to.

"What?" Hannah gasped as she felt Borj moving again inside her.

"I have need of you still, *ku lei*," Borj groaned out again, kissing her deeply as he began moving again.

Hannah stopped thinking and just began enjoying the feel of Borj's body against hers. *No wonder my parents are always getting it on if it feels this good,* Hannah thought vaguely. She heard Borj's chuckle before he deepened the kiss and she stopped thinking about anything but him.

CHAPTER ELEVEN

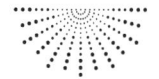

Life fell into a pattern over the next several weeks. Tresa explained Teriff finally, reluctantly agreed to send Terra to stay with Cosmos until the next mating ceremony which was in a few months. Borj's younger brother, Mak, escorted her and was going to stay for a couple weeks until he was satisfied Terra would be safe with Cosmos and on Earth.

They left the day before and Hannah missed the sweet girl already. Terra had spent a great deal of time with her, Tink and Tilly teaching them the language so they weren't dependent on the translators. She reminded Hannah of a female Cosmos in how smart she was and how she often got caught up in what she was doing. Hannah felt confident Cosmos would do a good job protecting the delicate young woman who was used to being protected by her three older brothers and one younger brother.

Hannah even met Derik, who was allowed to accompany Mak but only for a few days. He was still in training as a warrior and could not miss many lessons. Mak promised to work with him while they were gone. Derik was full of himself because he had already been to Earth and wanted to introduce Mak to some of the sights; namely beer and babes.

During this time, Hannah even got over feeling embarrassed about her parents making out in all the hallways since Tink and J'kar were just as bad about doing it. Hell, she even caught Tresa and Teriff a couple of times! Although, she had to admit she could totally appreciate where they were coming from now that she had a taste of the passion pie. It was almost impossible for her to not touch Borj whenever they were near each other. Near meaning if he was anywhere she could get her hands on him. Hannah couldn't believe how much she had changed over just a few short weeks. She loved the sense of freedom and power she felt. It was like she found a missing piece to her soul.

Unfortunately, getting her hands on Borj didn't come as often as she would like as Borj attended a number of meetings during the day. During this time, Hannah took the opportunity to explore the palace and outside gardens learning the layout and photographing everything from the daily lives of the people who lived and worked there to the different plants and animals she saw.

Her mom helped her set up a developing system in one of the smaller rooms in her and Borj's living quarters so she could continue her work. Hannah gazed out the window, knowing she would need to talk to Borj soon about exploring further afield but for now she could wait.

Things changed late last night when Borj came in growling under his breath. It seemed members of the Eastern Mountain Clan sent a group of representatives to meet with Teriff and the council of Elders who ruled in regards to Tink. Borj suggested Hannah might want to stay close to their living quarters until the group left again. He explained they wanted to know if the information they received from Bachman was correct.

Of course, once Tink and Tilly found out a bunch of hot guys were sniffing around wanting to know more about Tink they couldn't resist sneaking out. So, the next morning after the guys left, Hannah, Tink, and Tilly snuck out to see what these other warriors looked like. Borj didn't say anything to Hannah except to stay close to their living quarters. She considered since she wasn't leaving the palace that meant close to her.

J'kar, on the other hand, gave dire threats to Tink if he caught her out of their living quarters. Tink crossed her fingers and promised she would be good. Her look of innocence made J'kar frown all that much more. Tink pointed out to Hannah, she said she would be good.

She never said she would stay in their living quarters and never said what she would be good, so according to her and their mom, she was covered. Hannah had rolled her eyes at that logic and figured since she was the only sane one of the three she better go to help them when - not if - but when they got in trouble. She knew her sister and mom too well not to expect anything to happen.

J'kar had been so determined to make sure Tink didn't sneak out he programmed the door to their living quarters to be locked and only opened by him or the guard in case of an emergency. What he didn't plan on was Tilly, Tink, and RITA working together. Tilly distracted the guard while Tink and RITA hacked into the command sealing the door. Within minutes, Tink was free and the guard was unknowingly guarding an empty room. Tilly and Tink sought out Hannah and that was how the three of them ended up hiding behind a couple of large planters in the Council Chambers, having snuck in before everyone arrived.

Hannah looked through the plants curiously as a large group of huge men wearing some type of leather pants, high boots, and leather vests came into the room. They looked different not only in the way they dressed, but also in that their hair was longer and braided in thin braids. Several had weapons and when the guards approached them Hannah held her breath when it looked like a Mexican standoff was about to happen. It was only a sharp order from Teriff that caused all the men to back off with just a little more posturing.

Tilly rolled her eyes and mouthed 'men'. Tink and Hannah bit back a giggle at their mom. She was going to get them all caught! Hannah turned her head to look back at what was going on.

"What is the purpose of this visit?" Teriff said, standing tall in front of the other men.

Hannah's eyes darted to her mother who was cupping herself and showing Teriff must have a huge set of steel balls to stand up to the six huge men standing in front of him. Hannah barely smothered her chuckle, but Tink's escaped with a tiny squeak. One of the warriors in the back turned slightly and all three women froze. Hannah saw him raise his nose and sniff the air. She had seen similar behavior in the male lions and gorillas she would photograph.

Hannah barely let her hand move to show her mom and Tink to hold still. If he continued, they might need to beat a hasty retreat. It would be tricky, but there was a side door about six feet from them that led to another corridor according to RITA's schematic of the palace. RITA was going to monitor them in case they needed help escaping. She would unlock and lock doors as needed.

Hannah let out a sigh of relief when the warrior turned back around when the man next to him said something. Hannah leaned forward slightly so she could listen.

"You have a female from a different species that one of you has been able to bond with successfully. You will share where her planet is with us," the broadest warrior said in a smooth voice.

Hannah shivered as his deep, rich voice rolled over her. He could have been a voice-over to any sexy movie. His voice alone made a girl think of cold sheets, hot skin, and sweaty bodies tangled together. Hannah looked at her mom who was fanning herself with a 'wow' expression on her face. Tink didn't help when she licked one of her fingers and made a slight sizzling sound. *On second thought,* Hannah thought, *it was going to be Tink that got them caught!*

Tink knelt down when J'kar's eyes suddenly flashed to the planter where she was hiding with Tilly. Hannah watched as his eyes narrowed dangerously. *Uh oh, Tink wasn't as good at hiding her thoughts as Hannah was.* Hannah bit back a grin as she saw his face darken and his lips tighten. Hannah glanced at Tink, but she was just grinning dangerously. *Double uh oh.*

Hannah's eyes swung to J'kar's face just in time to see him flush a dark red and his eyes glaze slightly. Whatever Tink was thinking it was definitely having an effect on him. Hannah let her gaze wander over to Borj wondering if she could do that to him as well. She let a picture of her sucking on his cock, long and slow with his hands tangled in her long hair form in her mind, and watched his face.

Borj stiffened as a crystal clear image flowed into his mind of

Hannah on her knees in front of him. He fought the surge of blood to his cock but it was no use as the images of her slowly sliding his thick length into her mouth caused him to jerk as if it was really happening.

He shifted slightly as he felt the pressure building. His eyes drooped to half closed as the images changed to show her moving over him to allow him to feast on her while she continued to pleasure his cock with her mouth. His face flushed with need as he fought back a groan. Just as suddenly the image vanished, leaving him hard and unsatisfied. He couldn't quite keep the low curse from escaping as his eyes swung around the room frantically.

Hannah bit down hard on her knuckles to keep from laughing out loud. *Yup, she could do it too, if the look on Borj's face was anything to go by.* Hannah glanced at Tink and her mom and saw both of them grinning at her with their thumbs up in triumph. Hannah blushed and turned back to look at the group again. *If she wasn't careful, she was going to be the one to get them caught,* she thought with a huge grin. She hadn't had this much fun in… she couldn't remember!

The man in the back looked at both Borj and J'kar before turning to look over his shoulder again. Hannah made sure she was hidden, but got the weirdest feeling he knew she was there as his eyes continued to stare at the planter she was hiding behind.

Hannah realized she was missing a good portion of the discussion and forced herself to behave. RITA was going to have to fill in the missing parts. They were having her record what was going on for them, as well.

Teriff looked at Merrick for a long moment before replying. As leader of the Eastern Mountain Clan, Teriff knew he needed to be careful with how he handled this situation. Merrick could be one mean son-of-a-bitch when he was in a good mood. The clan was small but powerful. Their skills in the mountains and high trees were unprecedented. They were a valuable ally.

"What of the human male? He is dangerous. He killed two of my warriors. I want him delivered to us," Teriff responded coldly.

"He still has his purpose. When we are done with him, I will turn him over," Merrick said arrogantly. "Where did you get the female?"

"That information cannot be shared at this time," J'kar responded, stepping up next to his father.

"Why? We wish to see her. I, personally, doubt that she is real. I have never seen a creature such as her in all my travels to other systems. I believed this male is lying. But..." Merrick said with a raised eyebrow and a cruel twist to his lips that could be considered a smile. "... Now I wonder. I want to see this female for myself."

J'kar's fist clenched as he fought back the urge to challenge Merrick. He knew the warrior was baiting him, but the thought of exposing his tiny mate to such a threat caused his blood to boil. What infuriated him even more was the knowledge his tiny mate was probably closer than he would like right now.

He fought back the urge to clear everyone out of the room so he could find where she was hiding. Then, he might not be able to beat her ass right now, but he could definitely tie her up! J'kar let his eyes flicker around the room briefly again narrowing on the large planters towards the back.

"That is not possible," Teriff answered in a low voice. "The male you have not only killed two of my warriors, but tried to kill my son's bond mate. You know the penalty for that. He struck her and stabbed her repeatedly. If not for their bond, she would have died. What warrior would protect another who would harm a defenseless female of any species?"

Merrick's eyes grew dark at not only the insult to his clan but at the thought of a male attacking a female and harming her so badly. The human male said nothing about killing any Prime warriors or harming the female in the holovid. Merrick would deal with the human male who thought to take advantage of him. His jaw tightened as he fought back his own annoyance.

"Answer this question. Was one of your warriors able to bond with a female from a different species? If so, are you prepared to share this knowledge with other clans?" Merrick asked Teriff.

Merrick watched as several of the other council members leaned in to talk in hurried whispers. He already knew the answer. He just wanted a chance to see the female. It was hard to see from the grainy image and the angle if the female species was worth pursuing. Personally, he was still skeptical, but for the sake of his clan, he made the decision to come see for himself if what was on the holovid was true. Just the thought of what the female had said made him shift in discomfort as his cock swelled. He let out a low growl of frustration.

"Merrick," a soft voice came from behind him.

Merrick let his head turn slightly to look at one of his younger cousins. "What?" he practically snarled under his breath.

Core stepped closer so he couldn't be overheard. "There is something at the back of the room hidden. I do not know if it is a trap, but I sense something and cannot figure out what it is but my senses tell me something is there," Corman said in a deep, hushed voice.

Merrick looked at the members of the 'Tag Krell Manok clan. He saw both of Teriff's sons looking fiercely towards the back and conversing in aggravation. Yes, he felt it earlier too, but was distracted by the way Teriff stiffened when he demanded the female be presented.

Merrick nodded to Core. "Be prepared to fight," Merrick growled out.

"Merrick," Teriff said impatiently waving one of the councilmen back from him as the man continued to argue. "If you present the human male to us, we will allow you to see the female. Understand, she is already bonded and cannot be taken. Your request for more information will be discussed at that time."

Merrick growled at Teriff taking a menacing step forward. "You think you can dangle a leaf in front of us and we will accept your offer? You offer nothing! If you had the female you would present her! You have nothing! I want to see the female now!" Merrick said with a snarl.

J'kar moved in front of Teriff going chest to chest with Merrick. "You will stand down," J'kar snarled back moving into a defensive position in front of his father. Borj moved in beside J'kar baring his teeth which had come down at Merrick's aggression towards their father and leader.

Merrick's men moved out into a defensive stance. Hannah watched with growing concern. She had seen this type of aggression often and it almost always ended with some type of struggle, even if it was just a small one for show. She didn't understand why males of any species felt like violence was the only way to demonstrate how strong and macho they were.

Hannah focused on the posture of each male trying to see which would be the one to make the first move. She knew it wouldn't be the tall, muscular man standing chest to chest with J'kar. It wouldn't be J'kar or Borj either. Her eyes flicked to one of the men in the back. He was young and moving his feet just a little in impatience. He didn't understand the rules yet. He could be the one to make the first move.

Her eyes searched where he was looking. He was glaring at one of the guards who was staring him down. His pride was being challenged by the older guard. Hannah's eyes flickered around to the others. The councilmen would not be a problem, but the guards were getting antsy. Borj, J'kar and Teriff were focusing on the huge male in front of them. Shit was about to hit the fan.

Hannah glanced at her sister and mom. Tilly looked at Hannah with a grin. Hannah fought back a snarl of her own. Her mom would think a brawl in a council chamber would be fun. Hannah shook her head. Tink looked at Hannah and rubbed her fist into her hand. She didn't like the big oaf messing with her man. Hannah's eyes widened when she realized it wasn't the young warrior, the guard or anyone else who was going to make the first move but her little sister. Oh shit! Hannah tried to motion for her mom to grab Tink, but it was too late.

Hannah moved at the same time as Tink did. The moment the huge man went to grip J'kar, Tink let loose the most god-awful warrior cry and took off as fast as her tiny body could move. Tilly just shrugged her shoulder and let out a war cry of her own before following her youngest daughter into the middle of hell.

The moment Merrick put his hands on J'kar he could feel the change in the room. A loud war cry unlike anything he ever heard echoed around the room. He would have closed his eyes, but that would be fatal. Instead, he prepared for a good ass-kicking, preferably someone other than his own. He ducked as J'kar swung his fist listening as his second in command was hit. The war cry in the back of the room was followed by a second one.

He moved with lightning speed moving around and throwing a

low punch into J'kar's ribs. He heard the grunt and felt the pain radiate through his fist as it connected with J'kar. A moment later a return punch knocked him back several steps. By now, six Eastern Mountain Clan members were in a knockdown fight with a dozen members of the 'Tag Krell Manok clan, including their ruler and his sons.

Merrick was about to take another swing when something small and vicious jumped on his back, wrapping its arms around his neck and biting down on his ear with a vicious tug. He swung around trying to knock it off, but it was wrapped around him so tightly he couldn't shake it. He howled in pain as a set of teeth clamped down again on his ear and a set of hands covered his eyes blinding him.

As he reached up to pull the thing off of him another came up under his arm and hit him in the groin. His knees buckled as the creature on his back continued to scream curses in his ringing ears. He was about to get back up when something crashed down over his head and everything went dark.

CHAPTER TWELVE

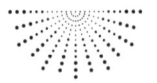

Merrick came to slowly with a groan. He was going to kill someone. He didn't care who it was but he was going to kill someone just for the hell of it. He could hear voices around him. It sounded like he wasn't the only one who was furious. The male's voice was raised in anger. Loud curses, threats, and promises of grievous torture were echoing throughout the room.

Merrick opened his eyes slowly. He stared up at his younger cousin and his second in command with a frown. Why were there two of each of them? Slowly the images blended until there was only one of each. Core helped him sit up. Merrick moaned as he felt the knot on the back of his head.

"Who hit me?" Merrick growled out dangerously. "I'm going to kill the bastard."

Core grinned, making Merrick growl out even more dangerously. "You might want to wait before you kill your attacker," Core said quietly nodding to where J'kar was stomping back and forth in front of a bench.

Merrick's frown turned to puzzlement, then wonder as he saw what his younger cousin was nodding to. On the bench sat three of the most tiny, unusual females he ever saw. They had similar coloring and looked somewhat alike, but there were also dramatic differences.

Two were very small. One was a little older than the others, but still just as enchanting. Her light brown curls in a disarray around her head as she looked on with a bored expression while J'kar yelled.

The other tiny one looked like a younger version of the first female. She was looking on with amusement as J'kar continued yelling threats at her. She actually looked like she was enjoying his ranting and not in the least intimidated by him. She was sitting swinging her legs back and forth.

The third one was taller than the other two and had a long braid down her back. She had a dark frown on her face and her arms were crossed in front of her. Merrick's eyes flickered to Borj who was standing next to her with a frown on his face.

"But..." The tiny female kept trying to say something. "But..."

"There is no 'but'..." J'kar snarled out at her. "I ordered you to stay in our living quarters! I locked you in! You disobeyed me. You will be punished for that."

The tiny female jumped to her feet at that. Merrick and the rest of his warriors watched in fascination as one by one each of the females stood up and faced the furious warriors surrounding them. None of them seemed afraid. None of them seemed to even be aware of what could happen.

If anything, the warriors now appeared to be a little nervous. A door opened in the back of the chamber and another male resembling the human male they had at one of their camps came hurrying in. He took the older woman in his arms in a brief hug before moving to stand beside her.

"You try to punish me, mister, and I'll... I'll make your life totally miserable! I was just trying to protect you and this is how you treat me! Like I'm... like I'm nothing but a pain in your ass. I just wanted..." The tiny female's voice faltered and a loud wail could be heard as she started crying. "Now look wh... what you made me do again."

The older female moved forward quickly and wrapped her arms around the tiny female comforting her. A few murmured words and the human male and the two smaller females moved down the corridor. J'kar watched them leaving in frustration and worry before he finally said a muttered curse under his breath and quickly followed them. Merrick watched in disbelief as J'kar gently picked up the female, cradling her in his arms. Whatever he said to her must have made her happy as she looked up at him and gave him a passionate kiss before snuggling back into his arms.

"Did you see that?" Core asked in a hushed voice.

His eyes swung to the taller female. He recognized her scent now. It was the one he smelled earlier when he thought something was behind them. There had been… the females. She was still much smaller than him. He watched as whatever the male next to her said seemed to make her angry. She tossed her head and glared up at him. The male bit back a curse before he reached for her. She pulled away from him, turning and walking stiffly away followed by two guards.

The male would have followed her, but Teriff called him. Core watched as the male looked first at the female before turning back to Teriff reluctantly. Core smiled. If he was her mate, he should keep a better eye on her. From the looks, she was not happy with him either. Perhaps, she would be interested in a different mate.

Merrick stood up slowly. "Which one attacked me? I need to return the favor of a pounding head," Merrick said with a grimace as he rubbed his ear and groin at the same time. "And by *hockta balmas*, who bit me?!"

Core laughed. "The one that bit you was the tiny female carried out of here. The other tiny one hit you between the legs, bringing you to your knees while the tall one hit you over the head with the planter. They then turned on the rest of us. I have never seen anything like it. Between the three of them, they were able to take out two more of our men before Teriff and his sons grabbed them," Core said with a glint in his eyes. "I want the tall female, Merrick. She could tell us where other females are."

Merrick's eyes narrowed. He did not like the idea of taking a female against her will but the needs of his clan weighed heavily on him. Teriff refused to tell them where the female's planet was and the human male couldn't tell them anything except it was called Earth.

He did not know how he ended up on board the warship the *Prime*

Destiny. All he said was Earth females liked to be taken against their will and made to be submissive. It was the only way they would accept a male. Merrick found that hard to believe considering what he just witnessed, but he did not know enough about the customs of this species to question the male. Perhaps, as Core pointed out, the female could tell them more.

"Why not the smaller female?" Merrick asked quietly, looking at where Teriff, Borj and the councilmen were quietly talking.

"I heard she was breeding. The one called J'kar yelled at her for endangering their younglings. He said younglings as in more than one," Core said with a small grin. "I have never heard of a female breeding more than one youngling at a time."

"Be quick. I will meet you on the edge of the forest. Make sure she is not harmed. Until we know she is bonded to any of the males, I want her to remain untouched. I want to learn more. I do not like that the human male did not tell us everything," Merrick growled out quietly.

Core nodded. Two of the other warriors left with him. Merrick watched them go with a sense of warning. Something wasn't right. He needed more information and he needed it now. He looked at Borj who was watching Core and his other two warriors with a frown. Borj's eyes turned to Merrick and narrowed.

Borj moved towards Merrick determinedly. "The other female is mine. I have claimed her."

Merrick looked at Borj with a raised eyebrow. "She did not seem happy with your claim."

"It does not matter what it appeared like," Borj said fiercely waving his hand in rejection of Merrick's observation. "She is mine. We have completed the mating rite. She wears my mating mark."

Merrick looked at the intricate circles on Borj's palm as he held out his left hand. He felt the sense of warning twisting in his gut again. Borj may be the quietest of the brothers, but that did not mean he was not as deadly as his brothers. Merrick thought of the tiny female in J'kar's arms and the symbol on Borj's. If he wanted his mate back then they would need to share the information they had on where the females came from. His clan was in desperate need of females. There were a few young females, but none of claiming age.

He would do what was necessary to bring hope to the males of his clan.

"You have found a mate and you would deny others the chance?" Merrick asked coldly. "You know as well as I do that times are becoming more desperate. The men need to find a mate or they will begin fighting and it will be the end of all of us."

Borj looked at Merrick in resignation. "I cannot promise anything but I will speak with my father and the council. They are aware of the situation. We have noticed it among our own clan. There are extenuating issues I cannot share at this time," Borj said quietly.

Merrick noticed the slight hesitation in Borj's voice. He understood Borj's reserve, but he had already set a course that could not be changed. The female would go with them and answer their questions.

∽

Borj watched in frustration as Merrick and the rest of the Eastern Mountain Clan left after receiving a promise from Teriff and the council. They would consider their petition for more information on where the females came from. He hated his position at times. He wanted to go to Hannah.

He said things he shouldn't have. He had been angry and frightened when he saw the three of them come out from the planters. He knew she was just protecting her little sister, but all three females did not realize how dangerous Prime males could be when riled.

He still couldn't believe his brother's tiny mate jumped on the back of Merrick biting him while Tilly hit him in his manhood knocking to his knees allowing Hannah to knock him out cold with a small planter. They took out half of the Eastern Mountain Clan warriors on their own, including their leader.

Borj started chuckling. Actually, it was rather funny now that he wasn't so frightened. When Tink jumped on Merrick and bit him, then covered his eyes while her equally tiny mother hit Merrick in his groin all the warriors around them were stunned. They were used to meetings like this turning into a brawl.

They would beat each other senseless then go drink together afterwards. It helped to burn the frustration of not being at war or having a female available. Obviously, the females did not know that.

When Merrick pushed J'kar, Tink charged like a seasoned warrior protecting her mate attacking the huge warrior from behind. When Borj saw Hannah calmly walk up and break the small planter over Merrick's head, knocking him out before turning on another warrior and kicking out, sending him to the floor as well, he wasn't sure what to do.

By then, Tink and Tilly had sent another warrior to the floor in agonizing pain. That was when his father, J'kar and he decided they needed to protect the other warriors before a true war broke out.

J'kar, furious his pregnant mate was even in the room, did not help matters by yelling at all three of them. Borj rubbed the back of his neck. He did not do much better. He should never have ordered the guards on her or restricted her to their living quarters at all times. Her quiet response sent a chill down his spine. She looked at him with such a sense of betrayal he hated himself.

You promised never to lock me up. You promised I would always be free. Her sad words echoed in his head.

"Borj!" Teriff growled out in frustration. "Get Lan and Brock in here immediately. We need to talk."

Borj inclined his head before heading down the corridor to the portal room where both men seemed to live. He could have called for them, but he needed a walk to calm his mind. He found both men in the room. Their heads were together. He could not see what they were looking at but they seemed excited. He watched them for a few minutes before they finally looked up realizing they were not alone.

"So much for security," Borj commented, leaning back against the door. "It was unlocked and neither one of you even realized I was here. What are you working on that has you oblivious to security and danger?" Borj asked, pushing himself off the door and walking towards them.

"Miss October," Both men said with a grin. Lan held up a copy of Penthouse while Brock had a copy of Playboy. "They are different females. I have never seen anything like this!" Lan said with an excited grin.

"Where in the *hockta balmas* did you find those?" Borj asked startled.

"Tilly!" Both men said again. "She and Angus had us over for dinner. She showed us what necking was and the bases of love making. She said it is much like their baseball. She said as in the game with the ball, sometimes a male strikes out, only gets to a couple of bases, or if he is lucky makes a home run. Angus showed us first and some of second base, but he refused to show us any more even when Tilly started teasing him.

Instead, she said some of the articles in these documents might help. RITA scanned them and is translating them for us," Brock said as he stared at the image in front of him. "I want to copy this image for my wall."

Borj looked at the two men and shook his head. Hannah was right. His planet might not be ready for the Bell family. He walked over and calmly took the small stack of magazines from the men. He ignored their protests. He was afraid to ask where the other magazines were. He would have to round those up later. For now, Brock and Lan were needed in the council room.

"Father and the council need you. The Eastern Mountain Clan came about the females," Borj said. He quickly filled them in on everything that happened in the council chamber, including the females attacking Merrick and knocking him out.

Lan laughed so hard he had to wipe the tears from his eyes. "I will have to get RITA to replay that for me. I would love to see those tiny females putting Merrick in his place."

Brock laughed as well. Both men had been on the not so forgiving side of Merrick's fist at one time or the other, mostly after a long night of drinking. In truth, both men respected Merrick as being a fair leader of his clan. Gods know, few could outsmart the bastard in the forest and mountain areas.

On rare occasions, raiders and space pirates would try to steal from their planet. In days of old, it was the young and females that raiders and space pirates would take. They would use the females until there was nothing left of them and sell the young boys to fighting houses.

This was very rare now with their defense systems in place, but a few months back both men heard of a group of raiders who crashed in the mountainous region. Merrick quickly dealt with the few survivors, especially after the remains of several dead females who had obviously been tortured were found in the wreckage.

Borj walked down the hallway heading back towards the Council Chambers. He listened with half an ear to Brock and Lan discussing the different women they saw in the magazines Tilly gave them. He couldn't resist glancing over his shoulder once more as a feeling of unease swept over him.

He had tried reaching out to Hannah several times, but she had blocked him. He needed to figure out a way to slip under the wall she built. It was driving him crazy when she cut him off. It left a huge hole in his soul that ate at him until she opened up to him again.

He knew she didn't even realize she was doing it. She had built those walls at such a young age, they were a part of her. He needed to give her time and build her trust in him enough to know he would never hurt her. Borj sighed heavily. He wasn't doing a very good job of building her trust in him at the moment.

Brock and Lan both gave him a funny look when he let out a long stream of expletives under his breath. Both men shook their head in sympathy as they moved into the Council Chambers. Borj might be there in body, but it was obvious to the other two men he was with Hannah in his mind.

CHAPTER THIRTEEN

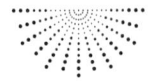

Hannah walked with her head held high and her shoulders back. She refused to let the weight of Borj's anger with her defeat her. She was used to being alone. Maybe she was meant to be. Tears filled her eyes, but she refused to let them fall. She should have known not to trust him. She should have known better than to trust anyone. Hannah was so focused on her internal turmoil she didn't recognize the warning in her gut until it was too late.

Hannah turned throwing an arm out behind her to warn the guards following her and twisted as two men came out from one of the alcoves. None of them saw the third man who came up behind them. The guards never made a sound as they sank to the cold, hard floor unconscious. Hannah was able to avoid the first dart that was fired at her but not the second. She looked down dazed as a numbness swept through her. She barely had time to call out one name before everything went dark.

Core caught the female to his hard body before she could hit the hard surface of the floor. He closed his eyes briefly as her sweet scent filled his nose. Core looked at the other two warriors with him. They quickly removed the darts and dragged the guards into the alcove. Moving silently to the window, Core waited as first one, then the other warrior jumped down. He gently dropped the female in his arms out the window, knowing the warriors would catch her.

He moved through the window, dropping down on silent feet to the ground below. With a nod, he took the female back into his arms. They moved silently, keeping to the shadows until they reached the thick trees near the high wall. They planned the move carefully knowing where the sentries were. They had just moments before the sentries came back around this side of the building again. It was a lesser used garden. Core and Merrick scoped the palace for several days before coming inside.

Core handed the female up to one of the warriors who had already climbed up the tall, thick tree. He followed next. The last warrior moved up the other side of the tree at the same time. Once at the top, they repeated what they did in the palace. This time Core went down first and caught the female as she was dropped into his arms. Within moments, they had vanished on the land gliders they used.

∾

Borj was listening to Lan and Brock give the council an updated report on the security measures and modifications to the portal they had made to make it more difficult for others to try to use. RITA was currently offline due to an upgrade Brock was making, but she would be back up shortly. She would be the first and last line of defense with several other safety measures in between to ensure the portals could not be used without proper validation. A self-destruct was incorporated at the first sign of anyone trying to hack into the programming.

Borj jerked when he felt Hannah brush his mind briefly. It was as if she reached for him only to realize it and withdrew again. He bit back a curse of aggravation. She needed to let him in. He reached for her, but all he got was the blank wall again. Maybe she needed time alone. A good workout might be what he needed to get rid of this feeling of unease that had started in the pit of his stomach as soon as he heard the Eastern Mountain Clan had been admitted to the palace. Borj looked at Brock and Lan with a gleam in his eye. It had been a while since he beat the shit out of both of them. Maybe it was time to remind them just how important it was to remain vigilant.

∼

Two hours later, Borj dropped down onto the bench wiping the sweat from his face and chest. Brock was lying on the floor of the training room, breathing heavily while Lan sat next to him with his head on his knees. Neither man said anything for a few moments.

"So, that was an interesting workout," Brock said, staring up at the ceiling.

Lan raised his head and scowled at Brock. "Workout? I thought it was a definite ass-kicking – ours," Lan looked over at Borj. "So, what did we do to deserve it this time? Was it the documents Tilly gave us? I mean, I didn't see your mate in those documents so I can't imagine you kicking it because we were looking at the other females."

Brock sat up with a wince. "I can't imagine it was for not locking the door to the portal room either. We were both in there. Tilly showed us the documents with Hannah in them, but except for the one where she was injured, I didn't see anything else that would have been so bad," Brock said as he rotated his shoulder and groaned.

Lan stood up. He reached down a hand to help Brock up and both men walked stiffly over to where Borj was sitting. They each grabbed a towel off a small table to the side of the bench and sat down, one on each side of Borj. Borj sat forward, twisting the towel between his large hands.

"She cuts me out," Borj said quietly.

"She cuts you out?" Lan said as he wiped his face. "What do you mean 'she cuts you out'?"

Borj sat back leaning back against the wall. "Out of her mind. I can't stand the silence. I reach for her and there is nothing there. The emptiness is suffocating," Borj replied, looking out over the training room with blank eyes.

"Have you told her how it affects you?" Brock asked softly. "Maybe if you told her it would help. She is human. She does not know of our ways."

Borj looked at Brock. "I said things to her I should not have. I hurt her."

Lan leaned back against the wall as well. "What did you do? I cannot imagine you doing anything to physically hurt her so what did you say?"

"I told her I was restricting her to our living quarters under guard until further notice. She would not be allowed out unless I escorted her," Borj said. "She reminded me I promised her I would never cage her. I would always let her be free."

Brock shrugged his shoulders. "She is a female. She should not be out unescorted. She will learn," he said, standing up and tossing his towel into a cleaning bin. "Go to her and take her mind off it. Bite her, if necessary. She will forgive you and if not, you can always tie her up until she does."

Lan threw his towel at Brock. "That will go over really well. I don't think that will help him at all. Apologize to her. Tell her you were just upset. I have been listening to what Tink and Tilly have been saying. The females of that world are strong and stubborn. They are also very independent. Angus often talks of the things Tilly does. He trusts her to tell him if she needs help," Lan said.

Borj looked up at Lan. "Angus told you this? That his mate asks for help when she needs it?"

Borj was silent as he thought back to the Council Chamber room. Angus had come in but he did not seem upset that his mate had been in the middle of a fight. He looked at her proudly and stood beside her and his daughters as if... as if he trusted them to know what to do and how to do it. When Tink started crying, he took both women in his arms and slowly walked them out.

"Gods, I have to let Hannah know I did not mean it," Borj said, surging to his feet. "I promised to never cage her and I will not."

Borj was almost to the door when one of the guards he sent with Hannah staggered through the door. Borj caught the man as his knees collapsed under him. Lan and Brock rushed forward, helping Borj lay the man down on the floor.

"They took her," the man whispered disoriented. "Not sure how many."

Borj felt a chill run over his sweat laden body. "Who took Hannah?"

The man shook his head as if to clear it. "Not sure. She tried to warn us, but something hit us from behind. Not sure what…" The man's voice faded as if he was still groggy.

"Look," Lan said quietly.

Borj watched as Lan turned the man just enough, they could see the small pin pick in his neck. Borj let out a curse as he pushed up off the floor. He slammed out of the training room and broke into a fast run. Reaching out with his mind, he called to Hannah.

Borj felt like his heart was being torn out of his chest when all he felt was a void of blackness instead of her warmth. He passed the other guard who was leaning against the wall. He vaguely heard Brock yell for more help behind him and the sound of running feet. Pushing against the door leading into his living quarters, Borj yelled for Hannah. Turning around in a circle, he ran his hands through his hair in frustration. He turned as J'kar and his father burst through the door.

Dropping his hands to his sides, he snarled out. "They took her. Those dead sons-of-bitches took my mate."

~

Hannah woke slowly. She could feel the drug still in her system. It made her feel sluggish and disoriented. She tried moving her fingers and found it was difficult to focus on them. She kept her breathing even and her eyes closed, letting her other senses take over.

She wasn't physically up to escaping yet, but mentally she was getting there. She just needed to listen and find out where in the hell she was and who took her. If she could get her hands on the darts they used, she was going to shove them up every one of the sons-of-bitches' asses. She was royally pissed she had been caught off guard. *That was another reason it was better to go it alone,* Hannah thought distractedly. *If I'm alone, I don't let shit distract me.*

Hannah felt her body being lifted carefully. She was being carried up a steep slant from the feel of it. She hoped whoever was carrying her got winded! She knew she wasn't a lightweight. Unfortunately, carrying her up a steep slope didn't seem to even begin to tire the bastard.

Fact number one, whoever took her was in very good shape. *Not good for me,* Hannah thought. She could smell the fresh air and what smelled like trees. Hannah let her eyes crack open just a tiny bit so she could see through her lashes. She caught glimpses of trees and dark shadows, but not much else. Not wanting them to know she was awake, she closed her eyes.

"Take her up to my home. I want to know the minute she is awake," a deep, smooth voice said.

It took everything in Hannah not to react when she heard the voice. She knew who had her now. It was the huge warrior from the council chambers. Maybe he was pissed she knocked him out. If so, he was going to be even more pissed when she escaped.

Hannah felt the arms around her tighten for a moment before the man holding her moved again. A moment later she could feel the change as if she were in some type of open-air elevator. *Going up.* Hannah thought in silent amusement. She might be able to use this to her advantage. Hannah felt the arms shift her slightly as the man stepped out of the lift. She fought her body's reaction to the cooler temperature as he stepped inside some type of structure.

"Who is she?" a young, feminine voice asked in excitement. "Are we keeping her?"

"Nadine, hush," an older woman said softly. "Core, who is she? I have never seen this species before."

"She looks like the male Merrick has, only she is not scary like him," Nadine whispered. "Is she hurt? She is very pretty."

Core chuckled. "Yes, she is. No, she is not hurt. I had to dart her to bring her here."

The older woman gasped. "Why would you do such a thing? It is not our way to take a female against her will."

"Nadu, she can give us answers. You know the males of our clan grow restless and more dangerous every day. The 'Tag Krell Manok is the only clan that knows where her planet is. She is not the only one they have. I saw two others. One is the bond mate of J'kar 'Tag Krell

Manok," Core said as he smoothed a strand of hair away from Hannah's face gently.

Hannah felt someone pick up her left hand. The hand was small, more delicate than the one touching her face so she suspected it belonged to one of the women in the room. A soft gasp followed as her palm was turned upward.

"You must return her, Core. She is already bonded. She has the mating mark. You cannot keep her. It will be dangerous. Her mate will come. You will bring war to our people. There are not enough warriors to fight against a clan as large or as strong as the 'Tag Krell Manok," Nadu said urgently.

Hannah felt the hand gently caressing her cheek and fought to hold still. She did not want to be touched by anyone else. She could feel the panic building in her as old nightmares surged to the surface. If he didn't stop, she was *so* going to have to kick his ass.

"I want her, Nadu. I mean to have her. Her mate turned from her when she needed him. He sent her away. I will never do that," Core said, looking up at his mother.

Hannah felt like she had heard enough. The man was sitting next to her and she could feel the knife attached to his waist. The moment the older woman released her hand, Hannah surged up swinging around at the same time and grabbing the knife. In one fluid move, she had her arm around the man's neck and the knife pressed hard enough against his jugular that she actually pierced the skin.

"Back off!" Hannah said coldly. She moved just enough to keep the man off balance. "I said, back off!"

The older woman gasped again and pulled a young girl, who looked to be about eleven or twelve, back behind her. Hannah glanced around the room. It looked like some type of bedroom. She pulled the knife tighter when she felt the man's muscles under her tense.

"I wouldn't if I were you," Hannah said softly in his ear. "I'll slit your throat before you would even know it."

Core froze at the cold, deadly words. He knew she would do it. There was something in her voice that made him believe her. He forced his body to relax. A part of him was cursing at letting his guard down. He had been so focused on her beauty and how small and delicate she was when he should have been remembering how quickly she was able to knock Merrick out. She was indeed a mate for a warrior.

"We mean you no harm," Core choked out as the pressure increased as she moved further back keeping him off balance so it was difficult to move.

"I'm sure that is exactly what the serial killer said to his next victim. I'm really not interested in what you have to say. I know what you want and you can go to hell before I give you any information," Hannah said coldly, never taking her eyes off the doorway leading into the other room.

Hannah wondered vaguely if the men here were close enough to humans to be affected by some of the moves she learned from her mom. After her attack, Hannah spent years training in martial arts. Her mom decided it would help her in several ways: The biggest way being to build her mental strength and the second to make her feel better about protecting herself should she ever need it.

Hannah decided so far the males appeared close enough to human males it might work. She could only hope she didn't kill the huge guy in her arms. Hannah let her arm slide around Core's neck and began applying pressure. At first, she didn't think it was going to work, but a moment later she felt him stiffen in alarm. He started to struggle, but she increased the pressure pulling him further back until he had to use his arms to prevent from falling.

"Shush, you will only be going to sleep," Hannah whispered in his ear.

Core was surprised at first when he felt the female slide her arm around his neck and press but he wasn't alarmed. It wasn't until his vision started to get fuzzy that he began to feel that something wasn't right. When she increased the pressure, he realized he was about to lose consciousness. He started to struggle but his limbs felt weak. By then, it was too late. He slumped just as her softly spoken words registered in his mind.

Nadine cried out when she saw her older brother's eyes close and his body slump backwards. Hannah slipped out from under the huge male and moved on silent feet towards the two females. She didn't want to scare the little girl, but she knew she might not have much choice.

"He's not hurt. He is just sleeping," Hannah said gently, looking at the little girl. Turning to the older woman, Hannah asked quietly. "Where am I and how far is it from the city I was taken from?"

The older woman looked at her son before turning her head to proudly look at Hannah. "As you said, you may go to 'hell' before I tell you," Nadu said.

Hannah couldn't quite keep the grin from her face. "I guess you're mad at me. Is he related to you?" Hannah asked.

Nadu looked at the unusual female in front of her and couldn't quite keep her own lips from curving. "My son," she replied.

Hannah nodded. "I didn't hurt him, but I don't have much time before he wakes. I just want to go back to my family. Surely you can understand that. Your son had no right to take me against my will," Hannah pleaded quietly.

Nadu looked at Core again before looking into Hannah's eyes. "You are our hope. He had no choice but to grasp it when it was within his reach. There is no way for you to escape. Lay down the weapon. We mean you no harm," Nadu said calmly.

Hannah shook her head. "I can't." Waving the knife at Nadu and Nadine, Hannah nodded towards a small door. "I need you to step through that door. I hope it is a closet otherwise I am going to have to tie you up and I really don't have the time to do that."

Nadu took Nadine's hand in hers and walked to the door. Hannah breathed out a sigh of relief when she saw it was a closet. Once both females were inside, Hannah grabbed a chair from the corner and wedged it against the door. She checked to make sure Core was still out and quickly ripped up some of the bedding to tie him up. Not as good as the tie straps, but it would have to do.

Pulling the cover over the window back, Hannah's breath caught at the beauty of her surroundings. There was a thick forest as far as she could see with a glimpse of the mountains surrounding them. She looked down and realized the 'home' she was in was actually about half way up one of the huge trees. Other homes were built into the surrounding trees.

Hannah saw dozens of huge men, animals, and other movement on the ground far below her. *Going down was out,* she thought in dismay. Hannah glanced up and noticed that further up the tree there was nothing but thick branches protecting the home. She let her eyes follow the line of several branches. If she went up, she could follow along them. Once clear of the 'village' below, she could climb down.

Hannah had no idea which way the palace was but she figured it couldn't be too far. She might be able to determine where she was once night came. She had spent several nights outside waiting for Borj to come back to their living quarters. She could use the direction of the moons rising and the stars to guide her.

Hannah tucked the knife into the waistband of her pants and climbed up onto the window ledge. She drew in a deep breath. Her arms and legs were still a bit shaky from whatever drug they used. She would need to be careful she didn't fall. It was a hell of a long way down. Grasping the top of the window frame she scooted along the edge until she could step onto a knot on the tree. Reaching out, she dug her fingers into an indentation and began climbing.

Hannah paused to rest at the top of the tree. She pushed herself up after a couple of minutes and began moving again once she was breathing evenly. She was walking fast along the branch when she heard a yell. It looks like her luck was running out. Either someone found Core or he was able to get free. She didn't pause to see what kind of excitement was going on far below her. She was more interested in putting some distance between her and everyone else.

She ducked down on a large branch several trees away as two thin black-looking bikes skimmed over the top of the trees. They reminded her of the types of vehicles she saw in movies back home.

Not that I've been to that many in the last couple of years, Hannah thought in sarcastic amusement.

She rose up again as they passed her and continued on. She was almost to the end of the branch when she felt someone behind her. Glancing over her shoulder, Hannah's eyes widened as the huge bastard and Core moved along the branch at a rapid pace. Damn, she thought for sure she could have gotten further.

Hannah threw caution to the wind. She started running as fast as she could along the branch. Her heart was beating as adrenaline kicked in. The old fears began swallowing her up as past and present collided. Hannah saw the vines hanging down from a branch slightly lower than the branch she was on. It was a good eight feet away and the possibility of her not making it was high, but she was too frightened to care.

All she thought about was the screams and looks in the women's eyes after they were brought back to the hut. Putting on a spurt of speed, Hannah leaped off the end of the branch, ignoring the loud curses of disbelief that followed her.

Merrick was furious when he returned to his home to find his cousin tied up and his aunt and niece trapped in a closet. How the hell did one small female do so much damage? First she knocks him out, then defeats his cousin?

It took precious time to figure out where the female went. He could not believe she could climb almost as good as his seasoned warriors. Few could use the trees as well as his clan. It was only the fact one of the skimmers sighted her that he and Core were able to catch up with her by using some of the roping hidden in the upper canopy.

He thought for sure they had her trapped on this branch. When she began running recklessly along it, he feared she would slip and fall to her death. He never expected her to try to escape by jumping to the vines.

Merrick looked at Core and growled out. "Where in the *hockta balmas* did they find these females?"

Core grinned as he watched Hannah swing down to a lower branch and jump down. "I do not know, but I want one!"

"Well, we have to catch the one we stole first. She is getting away!" Merrick grunted out as he watched Hannah jump onto another branch before grabbing a vine and sliding further down.

Merrick laughed under his breath. He decided he wouldn't mind having one either if they were this much fun. It had been a long time since he felt the challenge of the chase. He only wished it was with a female he could keep. He would have to let Borj know he was one lucky son-of-a-bitch.

CHAPTER FOURTEEN

Borj tightened the weapons around his chest and adjusted the ones at his sides. He was dressed all in black to help him blend in with the surrounding shadows. He looked over to his father and brother who were climbing out of the short-range shuttle behind him followed by Te'mar.

Te'mar looked grim as he approached. He looked at Borj's stony expression. It was not going to be easy trying to keep him from killing Merrick, he thought with a heavy sigh.

"Borj, I still think you should let me go in first. I can talk to Merrick. I can get him to release your mate," Te'mar said quietly.

Borj looked coldly at Te'mar. "If you do not have the stomach for battle, then leave," Borj said.

Te'mar's eyes narrowed dangerously. "This has nothing to do with whether I have the stomach for battle. You know I do. I have fought many times at your side. What I do not want is to see senseless killing that can be avoided," Te'mar responded harshly.

"He had no right to take my bond mate. I warned him she was mine. I showed him the mating mark. He knew what his decision would bring," Borj growled out furiously.

"He is responsible for his clan. He came to us looking for help and we gave him nothing but empty promises. What was he supposed to do? I do not approve of him taking your bond mate, but think of the choices we left him," Te'mar snapped back.

Teriff watched the exchange through narrow eyes. "As leader of the 'Tag Krell Manok, I will make the final decision. We will all go in. If they do not return your bond mate, then blood will be shed," Teriff said in a voice that told there would be no more discussion on the matter.

Borj's jaw tightened, but he did not respond. If Hannah was harmed in any way, he did not care what his father said. He would kill Merrick and as many others as he could before he died. Borj turned away and began moving swiftly through the forest. He opened his mind calling to Hannah but he still could feel nothing but the dark abyss.

"Borj," Te'mar said coming up beside him. "Merrick will protect her. I am sure he regretted taking her in the first place."

"Why do you protect him?" Borj asked as he moved through the thick undergrowth. "The real reason, not what you have given others," he asked, turning suddenly to look at Te'mar.

Te'mar had to stop or he would have run into Borj. His lips tightened for a moment before he looked out over the thick, lush forest surrounding them. He could hear the others moving forward, but was unconcerned. He knew if he could not calm Borj before they reached the village there would be unnecessary bloodshed. Torn between an old promise and the new one he made when he joined the council, Te'mar looked back at Borj in resignation.

"He is my older brother," Te'mar said softly.

Borj jerked back a step. How was that possible? He knew both of Te'mar's parents. They were bond mates. How could it be possible Merrick was Te'mar's older brother and no one knew?

Te'mar held up his hand. "Now is not the time or place to tell you the details. I am not even sure I have the right to. I can just ask that you believe that what I tell you is truthful," Te'mar said looking intently into Borj's eyes.

Borj studied Te'mar for a moment before he nodded his head. "As long as Hannah has not been harmed, I will hold my blade," Borj promised. "But, know this… if she has been harmed at all, I do not care who he is. I will kill him."

Te-mar nodded once before pushing past Borj to continue to the village, he called home long ago. Borj watched him walk away with mixed feelings. He understood family and the need to protect them, but it was nothing compared to his need to protect his bond mate. He had a better appreciation for the gut-wrenching torment J'kar felt when Tink was taken from him. Borj pushed his fear for his mate down. He had to believe she was safe.

~

Hannah frowned as she watched the group of warriors walk by staring at her curiously. She was pissed she hadn't made it more than a half mile before she was caught. She was better than that, dammit. She twisted her hands together in front of her, working at the ties. At least she hadn't made it easy on them.

The huge guy, Merrick, was sitting across from her scowling at her as Nadu pressed a cold compress to his forehead. Core was leaning back against a tree with a cold compress to his groin. Hannah had a feeling he wasn't going to want to spend time alone with her any time soon.

Merrick growled at Hannah when he saw her smiling. "You are dangerous, female. Does your bond mate know this?"

Hannah turned her gaze to Merrick and smiled innocently. "Yes. I knocked him out three times the first time we met," Hannah said sweetly.

Core groaned as he adjusted the cold compress. "And he still claimed you?" Core asked huskily. He turned to look at Merrick. "Do you think there are other females of her species that are not so painful?"

Nadu chuckled. "Why don't you ask her? You have her tied up to keep you safe now."

Hannah worked her wrists back and forth until one of her hands slipped out of the ropes. Even after she hurt them, they were afraid to tie her too tight for fear of hurting her. Hannah rubbed the red marks from where she worked her wrists back and forth. Pushing a long strand of hair behind her ear, she grinned as both men moved back away from her when she stood up.

"Actually, I am probably a little better at defending myself than most girls. My mom and dad made sure I could," Hannah said as her thoughts drifted to the reason why.

Nadu noticed the haunted look that came into Hannah's eyes and moved toward her. "Sit, child. No one will harm you. As soon as the men have recovered I will make sure they return you to your mate. Have you called to him?"

Hannah jerked. "Oh, shit! I was so pissed at him I shut him out. I bet he is really upset with me right about now," Hannah said as a flush ran up her neck turning her face a rosy red. "I forgot I could do that," Hannah added with a whisper.

Nadu laughed as she saw Hannah's face. "Call to him. Give him peace, child, or he will want to kill all of us."

Hannah nodded and closed her eyes. Reaching out, she called to Borj. *"Borj, can you hear me?"*

"I will be there soon. Have you been harmed?" Borj asked urgently.

"Let's just say I'm not the one sitting with the cold compresses. Remember when we met?" Hannah let Borj see Merrick and Core through her eyes.

"Perhaps, it is them that need be rescued," Borj's chuckle of relief sounded in Hannah's mind. *"I am almost there."*

Hannah opened her eyes and grinned. "He's almost here. He says he'll think about rescuing you guys."

Nadu and Nadine burst out laughing as Merrick and Core scowled. Merrick decided he liked the chasing part, but the catching left much to be desired. He gingerly touched the knot on his head where she hit him with the tree branch. His gaze flickered over to Core who was still looking a little pale. He would still prefer the branch upside his head than a foot in his manhood. He needed to remember if he ever came across another female of this race to be very protective of that part of his anatomy. It seems to be one of the first places they aim for when they attack.

Hannah watched a short time later as Borj, followed by a large group of armed warriors, came into the village. The few women and children in the village watched from the safety of the homes high up in the tree. Nadu stayed near Hannah but she sent Nadine, who protested loudly, back up to the safety of Merrick's home.

Hannah's breath caught in her throat at how sexy Borj looked. He was wearing tight leather pants tucked into knee high black boots. His upper body was only covered by a black vest, leaving his arms uncovered. He had two swords strapped to his back, several small weapons across his chest, and two guns of some type on each hip. His face was carved in stone as he entered the village. His eyes scanned the crowd of warriors until they came to rest on her. Hannah pushed by Merrick and Core running to throw herself at Borj.

Borj's eyes flared when he saw Hannah standing next to an older female. He watched as her face changed from nervous concern to outright joy at the sight of him. A moment later she was wrapping herself around him. He had no other choice but to clutch her to his hard body as she wrapped her long legs around his waist and buried her face in his neck. His arms tightened as he felt a tremble shake her delicate body.

"I'm sorry," Hannah whispered. "I promised to never shut you out and I did. I'm so sorry."

Hannah leaned back and looked into Borj's dark silver eyes. Without thinking, she pulled his head down into a deep, passionate kiss. She needed to feel him. Trust was a two-way street. If she expected to be able to trust Borj then she had to show him he could trust her in return.

Hannah felt Borj as he opened to her. She felt his fear and frustration. She also felt his sense of loss; the feelings of darkness and emptiness choking him at not being able to connect with her. The feelings frightened Hannah at first. She understood those feelings all too well. Ever since she was fifteen she had felt the same feelings. The only difference was she had learned to push them down deep inside her. It was the only way she was able to survive. She buried her feelings in her work, letting it show through her photographs.

Borj pulled back and looked intensely into Hannah's eyes. "I too am sorry. I made a promise as well to never cage you. It is difficult for me to not want to protect you. I have much to learn," Borj replied heavily.

Hannah let her legs slip down from Borj's waist as he looked fiercely over her shoulder. She slipped her hand into his and turned to follow where he was looking. A blush stole over her face when she realized how quiet everyone was and how they were staring in awe at her and Borj.

"What's their problem?" Hannah asked under her breath.

Borj glanced down in amusement when he saw how red Hannah's face was. "They have never seen a female be so responsive before."

Hannah frowned as she looked at Nadu. "Nadu seems affectionate," Hannah said puzzled.

Borj shook his head. "She shows affection, not passion. Prime females are not as passionate as your species. They do not seem to care much for the physical side of a relationship," Borj said softly as he began walking toward Merrick and Core.

Hannah frowned again. That was just plain weird. Maybe it was because she grew up with two parents who couldn't keep their hands off each other. What about Tresa and Teriff? They seem to like to be all over each other. Now that Hannah thought about it, bits and pieces of different conversations began to filter through her mind.

She remembered Tink telling her and their mom about the men's reactions on the spaceship she was on and how they were amazed at how she reacted to J'kar. She also remembered Tresa asking her mom a ton of questions about how to please a man and how he could please her. Maybe it wasn't that they didn't like it so much as they were never really given a chance.

Hannah jerked back to what was going on around her when she heard Borj growl threateningly. He was looking at the red marks around her wrist. He stopped suddenly and pulled her around to face him and lifted her other wrist up to inspect it. His eyes darkened and flames appeared as he raised first one wrist then the other to his mouth running his tongue along the welts.

"Oh god, that feels good," Hannah whispered huskily. "You can do that anytime you like."

Borj paused and looked at Hannah's half-closed eyes. "I am trying to heal you. I promised if you had one mark on you that I would kill

Merrick. I warned him you belonged to me. He will pay for harming you," Borj growled out.

Hannah laughed softly. "They didn't do this, I did. Well, they tied my hands, but that was only to protect themselves. I was the one who worked them free. They didn't tie them tight at all. I think they were just afraid I would inflict more damage," Hannah leaned forward so she was sure Borj was the only one to hear her. "Besides, if this is what happens when I get wrist rash I'll have to let you tie me up too."

Borj inhaled sharply as he caught the vivid picture in Hannah's mind of her tied to their bed. He felt his cock swell at the thought of her enjoying his restraining her. This was what J'kar was talking about when he told them about having to restrain Tink and her enjoying it. Borj felt his canines beginning to extend and knew if he didn't do something quickly he would take Hannah right there.

"You are dangerous," Borj groaned out.

"That is exactly what I told her," Merrick said coming up behind them.

Hannah flushed a deep red and an expression of irritation flashed across Borj's face at the interruption. That was the second time they both forgot where they were. Borj looked at his brother and father. Both of them had knowing expressions on their faces. Borj snarled out a curse before turning to confront Merrick. His fist connected with Merrick's jaw, sending the huge warrior to the ground on his ass.

"That is for taking my mate after I told you she was mine," Borj said fiercely. He then extended his hand and helped Merrick to stand up. "And this is for understanding why," he finished softly.

Merrick rubbed his jaw and spit out some blood. He grinned down at Hannah, who stood biting her lip. "I deserved that although I have to tell you your mate did a good job on me already. She said she knocked you out three times?" Merrick said as more of an amused statement than a question.

"Twice," Borj corrected. "I was still conscious the third time, but wished I hadn't been. She has very good reflexes," he said, rubbing his groin area.

Core choked out a nervous laugh while looking at Hannah. "I found that out the hard way," he said.

Hannah threw her hands up in the air. "That's right. Give a girl a hard time for defending herself. Might I remind you I was the one who was kidnapped?"

Core rubbed the cut on his neck while cupping his balls. "I might have kidnapped you but it was not without its difficulties."

Laughter spread throughout the large group of men. Soon, Nadu called to the other women to join in and a feast was prepared. Tales of Hannah's daring escape through the trees and her ability to take down an Eastern Mountain clan warrior grew until even Hannah had to laugh at the outrageous tale.

It was well after dark when Teriff called the head table to order. Teriff looked at the men gathered around. Te'mar sat next to Merrick and Core while J'kar, Borj, Hannah, and Teriff occupied the other side. Borj refused to let Hannah out of his sight or away from his side. They were going to stay the night as guests of the Eastern Mountain Clan as it was so late.

Hannah was enjoying sitting next to Borj. She loved being outside and the night air seemed especially fragrant. Her eyes drifted around the small village. Lights gleamed from the homes high in the trees while small campfires burned with small groups of men sitting around them sharing stories. The feeling of camaraderie and peace in the air relaxed her as much as the wine she was sipping.

"Merrick," Teriff said calmly as they sat around sipping a potent wine the clan made. "Where is the human male? He has a debt to pay for killing two of our warriors."

Merrick leaned forward with a nod. "Yes. After meeting the female I find many of the things he said hard to believe," Merrick looked at Hannah.

The human female was beautiful in the glowing light. He could easily understand how Borj was able to complete a mating rite with her. She was beautiful, strong, and courageous for all her smaller size. She was also passionate. The men of his clan deserved to be able to find a mate such as her. Their offspring would be strong and fierce. Merrick felt a ping of jealousy and envy that surprised him as he had never felt such a thing before. He knew what it felt like to long for a bond mate. Every warrior wanted one to warm his nights, and plant his seed. But, to have a bond mate who was also his partner was never something he even thought of.

Borj felt the growl rumble deep in his chest as Merrick stared at Hannah. "Down boy," Hannah said softly. "He is just lost in thought. Not thinking of kidnapping me again."

Merrick cleared his throat as he turned his gaze to Teriff. "He is under guard in one of our homes. I will have him brought to you in the morning. He has been treated as a guest until we discovered if he spoke the truth. Now that we know he does not, you may have him to do with as you please."

Core reached out and put a hand on Merrick's arm. He leaned in to him and spoke quietly. Merrick looked at Hannah, then Borj before turning with a heavy sigh to Teriff. He nodded once to Core.

"The problem of not having any females of age for mating remains. We ask for the right to know where the female's planet is so we may search for our bond mates," Merrick said heavily.

Before anyone could say anything Hannah spoke up. "You cannot get to it using a spaceship. It is too far," Hannah said quietly. She looked at Teriff who frowned at her before turning to Borj. "They deserve to know something. I've been observing their village all afternoon. There are only a handful of women here and they are all mated. I've also only seen four young girls while there are several hundred men. Even on my planet history shows when the population of males exceeds the number of available females there is war," Hannah said looking at each of the men.

"Are there not enough females on your planet?" Core asked tensely.

Hannah laughed and shook her head. "No, most parts of the world the women far exceed the men. There are always exceptions to the rule, but that is mostly in more rural areas or in areas where it is difficult to live but even that is changing. In the country where I live there is about a fifty/fifty ratio. Of course, that is for all ages, but females usually outnumber the guys."

Hannah fought back a laugh as Merrick, Core, and Te'mar let out a sigh of relief. "Then we can bring some here," Merrick said with a smile.

"Not necessarily," Hannah responded firmly. "There are things you need to understand. First, no one on my world knows that aliens exist. Second, if they found out said aliens did exist, it could be very, very bad. Not only would there be mass hysteria worldwide, but if any of you were caught, they would lock you up and probably take you apart piece by piece. On my world we have movies, similar to your holovids. These movies normally do not show aliens being nice guys. Third, if you just start taking females the local authorities are not going to be very happy and neither would the females' families. We don't get 'mating marks' when we bond. You would have to know if the female has a family, is she married, does she have children. There is a whole host of questions before you just take off with her. Not to mention, does she want to come and is she willing to give up everything she knows? Fourth, as I mentioned, it is too far to travel using a spaceship," Hannah explained carefully.

Core's mouth tightened into a straight line. "How did Borj find you then? How did Borj claim you? What of your family? How do you feel about giving up your 'world' and everything you know as you just said?" Core asked determinedly.

Hannah sighed and looked at Borj. "I said it is too far to travel in a spaceship, but it is not impossible to go to my planet. Borj came to the home where my sister was living. She was one of the small females who was with me in the Council Chambers. The other female was my mother. The man who came in later wearing glasses is my father. I…" Hannah looked at Teriff who remained silent, letting Hannah decide how much information she was willing to tell. Hannah looked at Borj who squeezed her hand in encouragement.

"How much should I tell them?" Hannah asked silently looking with concern into Borj's eyes.

"As much as you feel comfortable, I just ask that you not tell them where the portal device is until we have discussed it more," Borj answered.

Hannah nodded. Taking a deep breath, she looked back across the table. "What I am about to tell you must remain between us. I need your promise that you will not try anything stupid or act upon the information I give you without permission from Teriff or the council," Hannah said firmly.

Merrick nodded. "You have my promise as clan leader we will respect the knowledge you share."

"A friend of my family created a portal between our two worlds. He is the only one who knows how to do it. No one on my planet is aware of it, including our government. There is a great possibility of danger should it fall into the wrong hands. No one knew exactly what would happen when it activated. My little sister did so by mistake and found herself aboard J'kar's spaceship, the *Prime Destiny*, by mistake," Hannah said looking at J'kar.

J'kar continued. "Tink saved my younger brother, Derik's, life. We were attacked by a group of Juangans. They had set up a trap and we walked right into it. This portal opened onto our warship and Tink was able to kill the beast before it killed Derik. She treated his wounds and helped bring him to the bridge where Borj and I were.

The moment I saw her…" J'kar's voice broke off for a moment as he remembered the first time he saw Tink. A small smile curved his lips. "… The moment I saw her it was unlike anything I had ever encountered before. She seemed to glow. I tried to catch her, but she was too quick. She had never been in space before and was fascinated by it. But, it was when she grabbed my hand that I felt the mating rite."

J'kar lifted his left hand so the others could see the intricate circles on the palm of his hand. "I felt the force of it throughout my body as if I had been shot with an electrical charge. I could not understand anything she said, but it did not matter, I knew she was mine. Not long after, the portal doorway opened and Cosmos, the man who created the portal, took her from me." All the men saw the pain that flashed across J'kar's face at the memory. "I feared I would never find her," he said quietly.

"But, you did and you saved her life," Hannah said gently. She continued the story. "The man you have been protecting was stalking my sister. He wanted to rape her and kill her. He trapped her in a small room and beat her before stabbing her repeatedly. If not for J'kar, she would have died," Hannah said quietly.

Borj pressed a kiss into Hannah's palm as her eyes filled with tears at the near loss of her sister. "Human females are very passionate creatures. It was a surprise to us as we are not accustomed to such behavior from our females without at least releasing the mating chemical into their bodies. Tink shared many things with the crew when they became curious," Borj laughed as he remembered his own reaction to her 'things'.

Teriff laughed out loud. "Yes, much to my enjoyment. My mate is learning much and I am enjoying her lessons," Teriff said with a grin as he adjusted the front of his suddenly tight pants.

Hannah blushed. "This is really more information than I think I want to know. Tink is a lot like my mom, you ask and she gives you more detailed information than you really need," Hannah muttered.

"I liked the information she gave on the holovid," Core said with a curious smile. "But, is what she said even possible?"

"Yes!" Borj, J'kar and Teriff all practically shouted at the same time. All three had huge smiles on their faces.

Hannah looked back and forth before shaking her head. "I don't want to know what she told you guys. Something tells me I would be mortified."

Borj grinned wickedly and let images of what Tink said flow through his thoughts to Hannah. He watched as her jaw dropped and her face turned a brilliant shade of red that could be seen even in the glow of the firelight. As he continued, he felt his own blood heat as thoughts of doing them to Hannah began changing the images to their bodies entwined as he brought her to release.

Hannah's soft moan filled the air and all the men glanced at her as she tensed suddenly then melted against Borj. Sniffing the air, all the men groaned loudly as if they could taste her sweet cream.

CHAPTER FIFTEEN

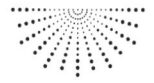

"You have to come out from under the covers at some point otherwise we will have to remain here," Borj said gently trying to pry the covers down from where Hannah had pulled them.

"I'm never coming out again," Hannah's muffled voice said. "I'm going to live the rest of my life right here and die peacefully."

Borj was finally able to pull the cover from over Hannah's still hot face. "I can't believe you did that to me last night!" Hannah whispered fiercely.

Borj chuckled as he rolled on top of Hannah's naked body. "I love how responsive you are to me," Borj said as he pushed Hannah's thighs apart so he could settle his heavy cock against her moist mound. Hannah moaned softly as Borj pushed his thick, heavy length into her hot pussy.

He had woken more than a half hour ago to find Hannah's hand gripping his cock tightly while she still slept. Thin streams of light were just breaking through the dark sky and beginning to shine down through the thick canopy above casting early morning shadows in the room. Sometime during the night their roles reversed. He found

Hannah curled tightly against his back, holding him while he faced the window.

Borj bit back a moan as Hannah's hand gently squeezed his fast hardening cock as she dreamed. Unable to hold back, he gripped her hand around his cock and rolled over until he was facing her. He loved watching as her eyes slowly flickered as she woke.

She lay next to him with a sleepy smile on her face before a deep blush darkened it. That was when he knew she remembered how their night started. With a loud groan, she jerked the covers over her head with a loud mutter about a painful death to all men.

∽

After Hannah's unexpected climax at the table last night, thanks to the images Borj sent to her, the men quickly called it a night. Hannah was too mortified by what happened to look at any of them as they made a quick exit. Borj swung Hannah up in his arms and hurried to Merrick's home. They were staying in the room she was originally placed in. Borj barely made it into the room before he set her down and pulled both their pants around their ankles.

He turned Hannah until she was facing the door and pushed her against it. Hannah had to brace her hands so she wouldn't fall with her pants tangled around her boots. Borj quickly thrust his cock deep inside her as she bent forward. His loud groan of need fired Hannah's pussy until she could feel the moisture running down the inside of her leg. She was already wet from the climax she had in front of all the men, as it was.

"Gods, Hannah. I love you so much," Borj murmured as he took her hard and fast. "You are the light to my soul," he groaned as her slick channel tightened around him as she came again.

Hannah's nails clawed at the wood of the door and she fought an unsuccessful battle to keep her loud cry of pleasure from escaping. Borj's own cries of release echoed Hannah's as he pushed in as far as he could. Borj held Hannah's hips tightly as he felt the last of his seed spill deep inside her.

Afterwards, he carried her to the bed and gently laid her down. He carefully removed her boots, pants and shirt before turning to the bowl of water on a nearby stand. Dipping a cloth in it, he cleaned her first before cleaning himself.

Only then, did he climb into the bed next to her, pulling her tightly against his body. He held her against him running his hand up and down her back until he felt her slip into a deep, dreamless sleep. Borj lay awake for several hours longer just enjoying the feel of holding Hannah's soft body safely against his own.

Just remembering what happened last night had him ready to explode all over again. *"You have nothing to be ashamed of. Last night was beautiful,"* Borj whispered as he moved slowly back and forth enjoying her tight channel.

"I had a bloody orgasm in front of a bunch of men, including your father and brother and you say I have nothing to be ashamed of?" Hannah thought with a groan. *"Obviously it embarrassed them! Did you see how fast they left?"*

Borj chuckled, then groaned as Hannah squeezed down on him. *"They left because the scent of your arousal caused them to become aroused. They all found a place to relieve their own needs,"* Borj said in a strained whisper.

Hannah looked up into Borj's eyes in shock. *"You mean they found other women? If J'kar cheated on my sister, I'm going to mount his balls on a wall!"* Hannah growled out silently.

Borj shook his head slightly. *"He would not betray your sister. He probably contacted her the way we are communicating now and found release together, even while they were apart. The same for my father knowing the way he and my mother have been ever since they met your sister. For the others, I cannot say. I am more concerned with what is happening now,"* Borj bit out.

"Oh," Hannah wiggled so she could wrap her legs higher around Borj's back. "This feels so good," she moaned out loud.

The new position forced Borj to push deeper into Hannah. Borj wrapped his arms tightly around Hannah, pulling her into his chest and began moving faster and harder. He felt his canines drop and knew he would mark her again as his. He heard Hannah's gasp as his teeth pushed through the skin on her shoulder. An explosion of heat engulfed his cock as the chemical moved through both of them releasing the hormones needed to prepare her womb for his seed.

They had not talked about having children, but it might already be too late to worry about that. In a Prime female, he could bite her thousands of times over a course of years and never impregnate her, but if Hannah was anything like Tink it was possible she was already breeding. He would need to remember to have the healer examine her when they returned to the palace.

It was over an hour later when Hannah followed Borj down out of Merrick's home. Nadu and Nadine laughed and joked about the lateness of the hour as they emerged out of the bedroom. Borj finally convinced Hannah there was no need to sneak off because of what happened the night before.

He promised her none of the men would say anything or think less of her. If anything, he was proud to show off how responsive his mate was to him. Hannah shook her head and muttered something about 'a male peacock and his feathers'. Borj didn't understand when she tried to explain what she meant so she decided to just let him strut his stuff.

Hannah watched as Merrick, Core, Te'mar, Teriff, and J'kar approach. They each had a grim face. A sudden flash of them 'relieving' themselves flashed through her mind right before Borj turned to face her. He pressed his lips to hers in a crushing kiss of possession.

"You should not be thinking of other men like that," he growled possessively.

Hannah giggled as she let her lips soften and returned Borj's kiss tenderly. *"You are the only one I want."*

Core groaned loudly. "Borj, can you not have mercy on the rest of us? I am still hard from last night even after seeking relief."

Hannah jerked her lips from Borj's and looked at Core darkly. "I didn't need that information, thank you very much. You are worse than my mom!"

The other men's faces cleared and they laughed. "Your mother is a very interesting person," Teriff said with a huge smile. "She has been of great help to my mate. I have learned many new things over the past few cycles."

Hannah rolled her eyes. "So much for promises," Hannah muttered under her breath.

"She did not break her promise, Hannah," Borj whispered wickedly. "She said she would not mention it unless asked. My father wanted your mother brought here so she could share more about human mating. Your sister, Tink, spoke highly of her knowledge."

Hannah's face flushed and she gritted her teeth. "She is NOT Dr. Ruth. She gets her knowledge from horsing around with my dad and the Internet. I wouldn't doubt if she doesn't make half of the stuff up!" Hannah hissed back quietly.

Borj slid his arm around her waist and pulled her closer. "I am happy with what I have learned. Are you not pleased as well?" Borj asked against the mark on Hannah's neck.

Hannah answered by jabbing her elbow into Borj's ribs. "I am not going to have another orgasm in front of these guys so knock it off. I'm going to go explore the village while you guys act macho. Call me when you are done," Hannah said sternly before blowing the effect by reaching up and gripping the sides of Borj's head and giving him a deep, passionate kiss.

Borj's dazed stare followed the sway of Hannah's hips as she walked off. It wasn't until J'kar punched his shoulder that he jerked back to the men standing around him. He shook his head to clear it.

"She really is dangerous and she does not even have a clue as to why," Borj said with a dazed smile.

Merrick shook his head. "Come, refreshments have been laid out for us. There are many things we must talk about. One of the things we need to discuss is ways of working together to bring more females here but that must wait. The human male is gone along with two of my clansmen," Merrick said grimly.

Borj's head turned sharply. "What happened?"

"I take responsibility," Merrick said heavily. "I did not have him locked up as a prisoner merely as a 'protected' guest. I wanted to talk to the female first before you came. I knew I would not have long. Then, she tried to escape and by the time we caught her, you had arrived. I had two guards on him but never told them to hold him as a prisoner. As far as I can tell he escaped sometime during the night.

Two other men are missing as well," Merrick finished looking darkly over the village.

"What are you not telling us?" Teriff demanded.

Merrick looked at Core, then back at the other men. "The two that are missing are dangerous. They tried to rape one of the women in our village. I explained some of the men of my clan are getting dangerous. It has been hard on them not having a bond mate. These two are brothers. They are part of the clan, but have lived in the mountainous region alone for many years. They have only been back in the village for a few months.

Several days ago, one of the women went down to the river to check the nets she placed. She was attacked and beaten very badly when she tried to fight them off. It was only her link with her bond mate that saved her. He was hunting close by with a small group. He heard her cry and came to her but not before she lost the youngling she was carrying. It was a girl," Merrick said quietly. "I believe the human male freed them with the same offer he gave to us, protection for more information on human females and where to find them."

Teriff let out a loud curse. "I told you he was dangerous. He must be caught as soon as possible. Do you have trackers on the human and the other two?"

Merrick nodded. "Yes, but it will not be easy. I told you the other two have lived in the mountainous regions alone for many years. They know it as well if not better than any of us, including me. Core and I will leave soon to join in the search. I do not want to take a chance of them finding any more females. From what you have said, the human male is just as bad. I have given orders to kill them on sight," Merrick stated coldly.

The men discussed different resources they could use to help expedite the capture of the three men. Even with the combined force of both clans, it would still be difficult due to the large amount of rugged terrain that would need to be covered. Prime was a large planet mostly covered in thick forests and mountainous terrain.

The thick cover would make it difficult to find someone who did not want to be found. Over the course of an hour they were not much closer to a solution. They were finally discussing possible ways to safely bring more human females to their planet when Nadine ran up to them.

"Merrick! Merrick!" Nadine came running up crying. "The bad men..." She cried gasping.

Merrick caught Nadine by her shoulders, kneeling down to look at her. "Breathe, Nadine. What of the bad men?"

"I saw them down by the river. They took the human female. She was not moving. They took her in one of the gliders," Nadine sobbed out. "They hurt Nadu."

Core swore furiously and took off. Borj paled as he followed. He had no doubts that the three men would hurt Hannah the first chance they got. He remembered Tink's battered body when J'kar brought her aboard the *Prime Destiny*. If not for J'kar linking his life force to hers, she would have died.

~

Hannah woke slowly again. She was getting really, really tired of people thinking she was placed on any planet just to be kidnapped. It was really pissing her off. She could feel the throbbing in her jaw where one of the huge males who came out of the forest hit her.

She, Nadu, and Nadine were walking along the river that flowed not far from the village. Nadu was telling Hannah a little about the history of the Eastern Mountain Clan when Hannah's danger alarm started blaring at her. The hairs on the back of her neck and on her arms were practically standing straight up.

Hannah put a hand on Nadu's arm to stop her and looked around carefully trying to gauge where the threat could be. Her eyes narrowed in on a dark patch of undergrowth about 30 feet or so from the path to the village. Hannah didn't wait to explain to Nadu or Nadine, she just reacted. If it had been just her, she would have taken a different route, but she knew neither Nadu nor Nadine would understand without her taking the time to explain.

Hannah turned towards the village and urgently told Nadine to run back as fast as she could. The warning in her voice must have been enough for the little girl who took off like a gazelle for the path. Nadu looked at Hannah in alarm when Hannah grabbed her arm and tried to hurry her back the way they came, as well. They were almost to the path when two huge men came out from the forest.

One of them struck Nadu across the face without saying a word while the other grabbed for Hannah. She was no match for the two huge males. When she fought, the one who struck Nadu turned and struck her across the jaw. That was the last she knew. Now, she cursed silently under her breath that she forgot to call to Borj. She was really going to have to work at this mind to mind thing.

"Yes, you do, but for now I forgive you," Borj's soft voice whispered through her mind.

"Help me!" Hannah pleaded silently. *"I really don't think these guys are going to be as easy or as nice as Merrick and Core,"* Hannah said desperately. *"They hurt Nadu! I tried to get to her, but one of them hit me while the other held my arms."*

"Nadu will be fine. The healer is with her. Can you tell me where you are?" Borj asked calmly. *"Can you describe what you see?"*

"No, I am still pretending to be unconscious. Something tells me it is best to do that right now. I can feel I am in some type of transport. We are weaving from the feel of it. Borj... I want you to know if anything happens..," Hannah said in a silent husky voice.

"Nothing will happen. You do whatever they tell you to do. I don't care what it is. Do not anger them. You stay safe until I can get to you. Do you understand me, Hannah? You do whatever you have to, to stay alive," Borj growled out in a low dangerous voice.

Hannah fought to keep her face a blank mask when all she wanted to do was cry. *"I can't make you that promise,"* Hannah said softly. *"I'm sorry. I will not let them..,"* Hannah couldn't finish.

Borj's throat tightened as Hannah flashed back to the women who were raped when she was younger: the empty eyes, the blank stares, and the devastation. He knew what she was telling him. She would take her own life if possible before she let them take her sanity from her.

"I will come for you, ku lei. Do not give up on us. Believe in me. If it gets bad close your eyes and think of me, I will be with you at all times," Borj said desperately. *"I will be with you, Hannah."*

"I love you, Borj. Just remember that. I love you," Hannah said softly before she pushed him to the back of her mind.

Hannah forced herself to remain still and to blank her mind. She could feel Borj deep down, but she did not want him with her if things got to the point of no return. She would not let him suffer with her.

Hannah felt the transport she was in slow and finally settle to the ground. She was being held in the arms of one of the large men who took her. He moved, sliding out of the transport with her still in his arms. She could hear someone else approaching even as he turned to talk to the man in the transport.

"Bring her to our home in the mountains. You better wait before you take her, Mazzum. I will kill you myself if you take her and she dies. She will satisfy both of us first," the deeply accented voice said coldly.

"Just get the fuck back if you want a piece of her, Amurr. Her scent is enough to drive me to take her now. I don't know why we cannot just fuck her here," Mazzum growled out.

"Because I want more than just one ride on her, you stupid *Tookey*. You heard the human male. Human females like to be fucked. He says they can take two or even more males at a time. If so, she will be able to take us both. If we do not kill her then she can be used many, many times until we find more," Amurr growled out.

"She is also the key to getting back to Earth," a new voice said. "I told you both. If you get me back to Earth, I can get you all the women you want to fuck. I'm a powerful man back there. You will have so many bitches you can have a new one each day if you want," the voice laughed. "You can use this one to experiment with. I can show you some really interesting things that can be done to a woman that will make your dicks so hard you won't be able to resist fucking her."

Hannah knew the new voice belonged to the man who almost murdered her sister in cold blood. She could hear the insanity in it. Hanna swallowed the nausea building in her throat as fear blossomed. If she didn't escape soon she knew she would never survive what they planned for her.

"Hannah, I need you to remain calm. You must help us find you. You must tell us what you see," Borj said firmly.

"The human male is here, the one that almost murdered Tink! He is insane, Borj," Hannah said, fighting to keep her body relaxed but she knew she failed when the male named Mazzum suddenly tightened his hold on her. *"The other one is leaving."*

"I know you are awake, female. Your bond mate will not be able to find you. If he comes, I will kill him," Mazzum said, squeezing Hannah until she gasped in pain.

"I will meet you at the falls by tomorrow afternoon. Remember what I said, Mazzum. I will kill you and the human male if she is damaged," Amurr growled out before closing the top on the glider.

Hannah's eyes flew open and she watched over Mazzum's shoulder as the glider lifted up and took off over the trees. She bit back a cry of pain as Mazzum's fingers dug into her waist in warning. Hannah forced herself to relax as her brain started to kick in.

"Borj?" Hannah called silently. *"They said something about a waterfall. I have to escape before the other man gets there tomorrow afternoon. They said you will never be able to find me where they are taking me and if you do, they will kill you. The glider…"* Hannah started to say before she stopped as agonizing pain exploded through her and she withdrew from Borj to protect him.

CHAPTER SIXTEEN

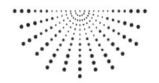

Borj was about to reply to Hannah when he felt a burst of pain so sharp it took him to his knee. J'kar grabbed his arm as he struggled to get back up. Borj drew in a sharp breath as the pain vanished as quickly as it appeared. He knew what he felt was from Hannah. The bastards were hurting her and she cut herself off from him.

"Hannah! Hannah, answer me," Borj demanded fiercely. *"Open for me, ku lei. Let me in,"* he coaxed gently.

"What happened?" Teriff asked furiously looking at his younger son's pale, sweat drenched face.

"They hurt her. I could feel it before she cut me off," Borj swore under his breath. "She will not open for me now."

Merrick came forward and put his hand on Borj's arm in support. "Was she able to tell you anything?" he asked quietly.

Borj shook his head. "Not much. There are the three men. She said the human male is there. They were taking her to their home in the mountains. They were to meet one of the men at a waterfall tomorrow. She was about to tell me which way the glider flew when something happened to her. I felt her pain before she broke off from me."

J'kar growled dangerously. "I should have killed the human male when I had the chance. When we catch him, I want him to understand the meaning of Prime justice."

Merrick shook his head. "It seems we have all under-estimated the human male. We have much to learn about their ways," Merrick added before he shook his head again. "There are many such places as your mate described. Many are small but there are a few larger ones. I will have the men break into groups of two. It is the only way that we will be able to cover even half of them. There is no way to tell until they show up. I do not want to risk any of my warriors unnecessarily. If they are found, I will have them follow the males until others can come. Both Mazzum and Amurr are extremely dangerous," Merrick grunted out.

Teriff shook his head. "The more we can cover the more likely we are to find them. I say we make sure as many are covered as possible. Whoever finds them can send for additional help. If the female can safely be spirited away, then she will be; otherwise, she will be followed. If we do not do this, there is a chance of missing her altogether."

"How many falls are there?" Borj asked quietly.

Core grimaced pulling up a holovid of the region. "There are more than two hundred in all in the region toward the mountains alone. I remember several years ago when I was a boy, my father and I ran across Amurr hunting. He would not have been far from his home as his kill was very large and he was carrying it. It was in this region. There are over fifty waterfalls in the area. I believe this is where we should concentrate most of our men," Core said pointing to a dense area. "It is very steep and a deep ravine with one of the main rivers for the region runs through the entire length. That is where the most falls are found."

"J'kar and I will take this section," Borj said, pointing to one of the larger waterfalls further up the river. "If we leave now, we can take one of the gliders a little over half way there. We will have to scale the rest of the way," Borj said, looking grimly at the terrain.

Core nodded his head. "We will cover the others from this point down," he said pointing to the holovid. "Teriff, you and Te'mar cover this area. The other males from the village and the ones that came with you have already been dispersed to these areas. There is still a lot of terrain not covered. Our only hope is the human male will slow them down," Core replied.

Borj turned without another word and moved toward the glider they would be using. Additional resources were on their way from the main Prime military, but Borj was fearful if Mazzum and Amurr felt threatened or were cornered they would kill Hannah. He desperately needed Hannah to open up to him again. He needed her to understand he was there for her, no matter what happened.

"*I know you are,*" Hannah's soft voice came.

"*What happened? Are you hurt badly?*" Borj demanded as he climbed into the glider.

J'kar slid into the pilot's seat and quickly activated the glider. Borj was so focused on his connection with Hannah he ignored everything else. He knew from the look his brother was giving him that he was aware he was communicating with Hannah again. This time he would stress how important it was that she never cut him off. It would mean life or death to both of them.

"*Bachman was wishing me his type of welcome. I'm going to be a little bruised but I've had worse. Luckily, Mazzum stopped him before he could do too much damage. I am going to play the 'helpless' female and hope it takes both of the men off their guard. Both are such assholes they think females are helpless little twits. If they let their guard down, I hope to escape,*" Hannah's soft voice replied.

Borj felt a shaft of fear go through him. If Hannah tried to escape and was caught none of the men would have any mercy on her. He needed to get to her. He knew she did not believe he would get to her in time. He refused to believe he would not.

"*There are many warriors looking for you. We will find you, Hannah. I will find you. You must not cut me off again. No matter what happens, do you understand? Our connection might be the only thing that saves us both,*" Borj said fiercely.

"*What do you mean...us both?*" Hannah asked hesitantly.

"*I told you once before, we are one. I cannot live without you and you cannot live without me. Our lives are bound together. It is the way of our people, my little warrior,"* Borj said softly.

Borj could feel Hannah trying to understand the magnitude of what he was saying. He knew deep down, she didn't really believe him. She was still thinking of him as a human male, not a Prime. Borj sent out a wave of warmth to Hannah to let her know he understood her confusion.

It would take time for her to truly understand what she had committed her life to. He did not care how long it took. He just wanted her back in his arms and safe again. Then, after Bachman, Mazzum, and Amurr were dead, he was going to beat the shit out of Merrick and Core for putting his mate in danger in the first place by taking her from the palace.

Borj felt Hannah's silent chuckle. *"Trust me. I think they have been punished enough. Besides, I never would have met Nadine and Nadu. Shit happens. I just wish it would quit happening to me! Things will work out, Borj. I have to believe that. This isn't the first dangerous situation I've found myself in. I am just fortunate that these assholes have no idea who they have taken. Come for me. I will hold out as long as I can but know this, if my gut says to take the chance to escape, I plan on following it. It has never failed me before,"* Hannah said fiercely. *"I won't cut you off, but I need to focus on where we are going. I'll send you images like I did before, so maybe you can recognize something."*

"I love you, Hannah. I will be with you soon," Borj pushed through to Hannah before he felt her withdraw from him again.

J'kar glanced over at Borj as he moved easily through the thick forest. "Was she able to give you any more information?" J'kar asked grimly.

"No. The human male hurt her but she claims to be fine. She will try to send me images of where she is," Borj said quietly. "I fear losing her."

J'kar threw a severe look at Borj. "You will not! Tink and Tilly will destroy us all if anything happens to her. Tilly already warned me if I did not bring her daughter back in one piece, she said quote "hell hath no fury like a momma pissed off'. I am not sure what that means, but if she is as dangerous as Tink when she is mad I do not want to find out," J'kar growled out.

Borj felt his lips curve. "Did you see how fast Tink, Tilly, and Hannah took out Merrick and half his warriors? They were amazing," Borj said hopefully. He looked over at J'kar who was weaving dangerously fast through some peculiarly thick trees. "Hannah escaped a situation such as this one once before."

The only sign J'kar gave at having heard Borj's murmured words was a tightening of his hands on the controls of the glider. "Their world is very dangerous," J'kar responded with worry. "I am concerned, we sent Terra there."

Borj couldn't suppress his bitter laugh. "Their world… what of our own? I thought bringing Hannah here would be safer, but she has been taken from me twice! Terra will probably be safer on Earth than here. Besides, she has Mak to protect her and Cosmos."

"That is true. No one can get by Mak. Out of all of us, he is the meanest!" J'kar said with a nod. "We are almost as far as we can go safely in the glider. I do not want to take us any closer for fear of being seen."

"J'kar," Borj said quietly. "I am proud to be called your brother. I want you to know this should things not go well."

J'kar snarled, showing his canines at Borj. "Nothing will go wrong except to the bastards who took your mate. If you even suggest anything different, I will personally kick your ass when we get your mate back to the palace."

Borj didn't reply. He did not want to express his fears that things could very easily go wrong. He knew what could happen to an unprotected female, even one who believed she was as strong as Hannah did. In truth, human females were much weaker than even Prime females.

"Bite your tongue, or I swear I'll cut you off and do this on my own," Hannah's voice snarled out in Borj's mind. *"J'kar isn't the only one who is going to kick your ass when we get back to the palace."*

Borj jerked as if he had been shot. He flushed a dark red. He had not meant for Hannah to pick up on his doubts. He could feel her anger in her heated words.

"I will happily let you kick my 'ass' as you put it when we get back to the palace," Borj chuckled softly. *"I apologize, my little warrior, for not having more faith in your abilities. I will not let such thoughts take over again."*

~

Hannah fought back a grin. Borj thought she had a lot to learn about Prime but he also had a lot to learn about human females. They were not the roll over and play dead type. She would have to take him on an assignment with her sometime and see how he handled it. Maybe they could do it as a vacation back to Earth. As long as they were away from most humans, it should be safe. Hannah let plans for the future guide her. It helped her keep her sanity.

Hannah gently rubbed her side where Bachman hit her. She could feel the tender skin. He had come up behind her when Mazzum set her down after he discovered she was awake. She was trying to focus on what Borj was saying to her while keeping a blank mask on her face and looking for some type of distinguishing landmark for Borj to find her and wasn't expecting him to attack her.

The bastard came up and kidney punched her taking her to her knees with a cry of pain. Once on her knees, he pulled her long hair back, exposing her neck to the sharp knife he ran along it. The tip barely caressed her skin, but it was enough to leave a long, thin cut about four inches long along it. Luckily, Mazzum's arm snapped out and took the blade easily from Bachman's hand.

Mazzum snarled at Bachman as Bachman raised his hands with a grin on his face. "Chill out, man. I was just prepping her for you. A little fear helps keep them under control," Bachman laughed at Mazzum.

"Amurr said no damage. You think he will not slit both our throats if the female dies? You touch her again without my permission and I will slit your throat and save him the trouble. We do not need you any more now that we have the female," Mazzum snarled out taking a threatening step toward Bachman.

"That is where you are wrong," Bachman said through narrowed eyes. "You and your brother won't survive without me on Earth. You need my contacts and resources. If you and your fucking brother try to go to Earth without my help, you'll both be caught and taken apart piece by little piece like lab rats. Only I can get you what you both want. This bitch is just a sample. There are far more beautiful women where I come from, isn't that right, sweetheart?" Bachman said looking at Hannah with a cold grin.

"Why don't you bend over and let him fuck you, Bachman? You're such a wuss attacking defenseless women you probably don't even have any balls for him to worry about," Hannah replied through clenched teeth as she breathed through the pain.

Bachman's eyes narrowed dangerously and he took a step toward Hannah with his hand raised. Hannah braced herself for another hit, but Bachman's fist was caught in Mazzum's thick hand before it connected with her face. Hannah watched in satisfaction as sweat beaded on Bachman's forehead as Mazzum squeezed his fist around Bachman's hand.

"She has a point," Mazzum murmured with an evil grin. "Amurr said I could not fuck her without him, but he didn't say anything about not damaging you."

Bachman's eyes flew up to look in panic up at the huge male towering over him. The sweat on his face suddenly vanished as he paled at the threat. Hannah looked on as Bachman suddenly realized that he was not in as much control as he thought.

Mazzum chuckled as he brought his other hand up to cup Bachman's groin. "Yes. I think I can see you bent over," he said before he released Bachman with a shove and bent over to grip Hannah's arm in a tight grip, pulling her to her feet.

"Move! Both of you. If she cannot walk because of the damage you did, you will carry her," Mazzum said coldly pushing Hannah in front of him until she was standing next to Bachman's pale, shaking form.

Hannah didn't say anything else. She focused on trying to see something other than massive trees and thick undergrowth. There was nothing else she could send to Borj that would help him. Even the direction the glider went was lost thanks to Bachman.

Now, she focused on keeping a light contact with Borj and not falling as they moved into the thick growth of the forest. Mazzum pushed them hard, often getting impatient with both of them when they stumbled, or began to slow due to fatigue. Hannah's gut was telling her to play the weak female and she was playing it to the fullest extent of her acting ability.

In truth, she could have been moving at over twice the speed they were covering, even in the thickest growth. It wasn't much different than some of the terrain she covered when photographing the mountain gorillas or some of the different plants and animals in the Amazon. Bachman was not fairing as well. There was no acting in his flushed face or heavy breathing. He might know how to survive in the urban jungle, but he wasn't used to the rough terrain.

Mazzum finally called a halt again when Bachman tripped again. Hannah leaned over looking at the ground acting like she was too tired to even stand up straight. Mazzum came over to her and pushed her down onto the ground roughly near a tree.

He knelt down next to her, grabbing one of her hands and pulled it behind her. He tied one end of a thick, coarse rope around it before tossing the other end of the rope around the tree. He grabbed the end and tied her other wrist so her back pressed tightly against the tree, forcing her to sit straight against it.

Hannah turned her head when he grinned at her. She bit her lip when he grabbed the front of her shirt between his thick hands and ripped the front open sending buttons scattering in all directions. Hannah's breathing increased as panic swept through her. She refused to look at Mazzum as he gripped the front of her bra and snapped the material freeing her breasts to his gaze.

Hannah couldn't pull her legs up because Mazzum was kneeling between them. She fought back a scream as he leaned forward, sniffing her neck and running his tongue along it. A fine trembling began as she realized her worst fear was about to happen and there was nothing she could do to stop him. Hannah couldn't quite prevent the slight sob that escaped as she felt a callused hand against her breast.

"You smell good even when you are sweating. I am going to enjoy fucking you. The human male says a female can take more than one male at a time. Tell me how I should take you. Tell me!" Mazzum growled in a soft, menacing voice.

Hannah turned her head and looked Mazzum in the eye. "I'll be dead before that ever happens," Hannah replied in a voice devoid of emotion.

Mazzum looked at Hannah a moment before he laughed out loud. "I don't think so, little human. I plan on having much pleasure with you before that happens," Mazzum said, squeezing Hannah's nipple between his fingers.

Hannah gasped as a cry of pain shot through her. Her lips parting in a cry of pain. The moment her lips parted, Mazzum crushed his lips down on hers, taking her mouth in a savage, bruising kiss. He continued kissing her and roughly squeezing her breasts as Hannah fought to turn her head.

When she tried to bite him, he bit her back hard enough to break the skin on her lip. Hannah felt his hard arousal against her thigh and his canines lengthen as he became more aroused. One of his thick hands wound around her long braid holding her head still while he ravaged her mouth and breasts.

When he broke the kiss, he was breathing heavily. With a curse, he glared hard into Hannah's stricken dark, green eyes. He pulled back into a sitting position and let his thumb rub over one of her bruised nipples.

"I will keep you. I like your taste. Soon, you will not remember your bond mate. You will only know my touch," Mazzum said thoughtfully.

"Never," Hannah said in an emotionless voice. "I'll never forget Borj. I'll never belong to you."

Mazzum merely smiled. His gaze swung around to where Bachman was sitting against a tree watching them. His gaze was glued to Hannah's bare breasts and he was stroking his cock through his pants.

Hannah looked over to where Bachman was sitting watching with a grin on his face and shivered. Bachman's eyes met Hannah's for a moment and she shivered again as she saw the lust in them. Mazzum must have seen the same thing. His eyes narrowed for a moment before he turned back to Hannah with a gleam in his eye.

"Perhaps, I should see how many ways a human male can be fucked," Mazzum said with an evil grin before he stood up.

Bachman didn't realize Mazzum's intent until it was too late. Hannah eyes widened as she watched Mazzum strike Bachman in the head, knocking him to the ground. In moments, Bachman was tied up and leaning over a fallen tree with his pants around his ankles. Hannah closed her eyes and hummed to herself in an effort to block the sounds of Bachman's screams.

CHAPTER SEVENTEEN

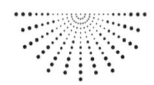

Borj and J'kar were traveling along the steep ravine Core had pointed out in the holovid. They were making good time. One group reported finding an abandoned glider almost forty clicks to the southwest.

One of the men was a tracker and was able to follow a step of single tracks but only for a short distance before they disappeared. The tracks were headed northeast towards the mountains. Core and Merrick were heading that way in an attempt to cut Amurr off. Teriff and Te'mar would back them up.

Borj wiped the sweat off his brow before reaching up to grab a large rock overhead and pull himself up. J'kar was about five paces behind him. Borj was just about up when he felt Hannah's scream and horror. He fought for calm as he pushed up over the ledge and rolled onto his back and closed his eyes. J'kar moved up quickly and knelt beside him. Borj shook off J'kar's hand as he focused on Hannah.

Borj felt her horror as Mazzum touched her and her revulsion as he kissed her. Inside, she was screaming and struggling to distance herself from Mazzum's touch. Borj's hands clenched into tight fists as he sent wave after wave of comfort to Hannah in an attempt to help her. He was breathing heavily as he felt the pain radiating through her as Mazzum pinched and fondled her.

"I am with you, Hannah. You are not alone," Borj said softly. "*Focus on my voice. Do not think about what is happening. Hear only my voice, feel only my warmth surrounding you. I will not let you go through this alone.*"

"I can't do this. I can't do this," Hannah whispered softly. "Take me away from here. Please Borj, take me away from here."

Borj's soft cry of torture escaped at Hannah's helpless plea. "*Come with me, Hannah. Let me take you with me to my home near our ocean. We will walk along the pink sands. You will love the wildness of the waves breaking along the shores. There is a small cove nearby where we can swim and no one will bother us. The water is warm and clear and you can see forever,*" Borj whispered back imagining he was brushing Hannah's long hair back from her face so he could see her beautiful eyes. "*We will watch as the birds and water mammals play. I will show you the sea dragons. You will love them. They are very colorful and love to play in the waves.*"

Hannah focused on Borj's voice as he told her about the sea dragons forcing the feeling of Mazzum's touch out of her mind as she wrapped herself in Borj's warmth. She could vaguely feel when Mazzum seemed to realize she had withdrawn into a place he couldn't reach her. She heard herself reply to whatever he said, but it wasn't until he actually stood and moved away from her that she came back to her surroundings.

When she saw what Mazzum was doing to Bachman she wished she could escape back into the world Borj had taken her. Unfortunately, Bachman's anguished screams, then quiet sobs made it impossible. All Hannah could do was close her eyes and hum while she tried to picture being back with Borj.

"We will get her back soon," J'kar said as he watched Borj's face twist in anguish.

Borj sat up and braced his head against his knees as he fought the devastating rage and pain racing through him. He felt Hannah's sudden withdrawal as whatever was happening to her became too much for her to block anymore. Her horrified screams filled his head before everything seemed to stop and a soft humming took its place. Her mind could not handle what was happening any longer.

Borj wiped a hand across his cheek, surprised when it came away damper than from just sweat. He stared at the traces of his tears on his palm. Closing his hand around it, he looked up into J'kar's sympathetic eyes.

"I am going to kill all three of those bastards. I seek the Right of Justice. It is my right to end their lives for what they have done to my bond mate," Borj said quietly.

J'kar nodded his head. "You will have the Right of Justice. I will let the others know," J'kar promised.

Borj rose to his feet with renewed determination. He listened as J'kar spoke into his comlink quietly telling all the members that Borj was demanding the Right of Justice. There was silence on the other end for moment before each group reported back in agreement.

None of the men would be killed unless there was no other way. All the men knew that a grievous injustice was done for a Right of Justice to be declared. The men's deaths would be long and brutal to justify the crime committed against a Prime male's bond mate or family.

Neither man spoke again as they continued on, moving even faster. It would be dark soon and they would have to move slower. Borj hoped on the one hand that with two humans, Mazzum would be forced to stop for the night. On the other hand, he feared what Hannah would go through if they did. His gut turned at what she had already gone through. A cold calm settled over him.

He promised he would be with her through it all and he would. He refused to allow the guilt or pain to take hold. There would be time later for him to confront it. Right now, his focus was on one thing and one thing only, getting Hannah back into his arms where she belonged.

~

Hannah focused on putting one foot in front of the other. Mazzum had untied her when it was time to leave. Hannah ignored his chuckle when she jerked the remains of her top together and tied it in a double knot. She froze when he ran his fingers across her cheek, refusing to give him the satisfaction of feeling her horror at his touch.

"He was not nearly as satisfying as I imagine you will be," Mazzum murmured.

Hannah simply stood still and waited. She focused on the pain in her wrists where the ropes had cut deep welts as she struggled to get free when Mazzum had finally left her and Bachman alone for a little while when he went to get cleaned up in a nearby stream. She could still see him, but he was a good twenty-five feet away. Far enough for her to get a head start.

Hannah had cringed when she looked at Bachman. He had a dazed expression on his face until he saw her looking at him. Then, a look of pure hatred and rage flared in his eyes, causing Hannah to work on the ropes even harder. She watched in horror as he rose stiffly and walked towards her. Hannah's head fell back against the tree when he knelt next to her.

"You are going to fucking get me out of this hell, do you understand? I'm going to kill that bastard and when I do, you are coming with me and leading me to wherever in the hell we have to go to get off this fucked-up world," Bachman whispered hoarsely in Hannah's ear.

Hannah looked at Bachman out of the corner of her eye. "And if I do? What will you do for me?" Hannah asked, looking back to where Mazzum was naked and washing himself in the stream.

"I'll kill you quick," Bachman said softly. "If you don't, I'll make what he did to me look like child's play. I'll draw every last scream out of you before I let you die."

Hannah's eyes jerked back as she felt the tip of a blade against the underside of her bare breast. He didn't press enough to break the skin, but enough to let Hannah know what he planned to do if she didn't cooperate with him. Hannah nodded her head briefly. She had a better chance of getting away from Bachman in this type of terrain than she did from Mazzum.

"What do you want me to do?" Hannah asked, looking back at where Mazzum was beginning to get dressed.

Bachman stood gingerly and stepped back around the tree so Mazzum couldn't see him near Hannah. "Nothing yet."

Hannah let her head drop forward as she bit her tender lip where

Mazzum bit her earlier. She was trapped between two insane murderers. If she didn't find a way to escape before crazy number three showed up she was totally screwed. She would have to hope a chance came soon.

Mazzum looked over at where Bachman stood with his head down and grinned. The human male was not so full of himself now. Mazzum looked down at where the human female was still tied to the tree and felt himself growing hard again. Her breasts were small but he found the darker tips very arousing.

He knelt down next to her sliding a knife out of his boot. With a quick flick, it sliced through the rope. His eyes narrowed on the raw skin on her wrists. He would have to wrap her wrists before he tied her again. He did not want to have her too damaged. He liked the feel of her smooth skin against his fingers. He let one of his hands brush her breasts as he moved to her other wrist.

He couldn't hold back the chuckle when she jerked her shirt together, tying it tightly, as soon as her hands were freed. He pulled her into a standing position running his fingers down along her soft cheek. He noted with satisfaction she did not pull away from him as he did it. His eyes narrowed on the long scratch along her neck and his eyes flickered to the human male who put it there. He would have to die. Mazzum would wait for his older brother, but even if Amurr was against killing the male it wouldn't matter. He would still kill him.

"Move," Mazzum said, nodding his head to the northwest. "We have much to cover before it gets much darker. You both move too slow. Female, if you cannot move faster I will carry you over my shoulder."

Hannah jerked her head in a stiff nod to let him know she understood what he meant. If she did not move faster, he would not only carry her over his shoulder but other things as well. Hannah pushed past Bachman without a word and started moving through the dense undergrowth with more determination. She did not want the bastard to ever touch her again. She didn't think she would ever feel clean again.

That had been over three hours ago. It was dark now and she could barely see her hand in front of her face. Mazzum finally motioned for them to stop and Hannah felt her knees tremble with a combination of exhaustion and fear. Mazzum nodded to Hannah to sit next to a tree. She reluctantly slid down the trunk barely holding in a groan of despair. Mazzum nodded to Bachman to sit next to her. Bachman flashed Mazzum a look of pure hatred before he sat down next to Hannah.

Mazzum chuckled as he quickly tied them both up. "You are not so demanding now, human. But I did not like the look you gave me. Perhaps you need a reminder of who is really in charge," Mazzum said with a ruthless chuckle as he tapped Bachman's face hard.

Bachman flinched at Mazzum's threat, but didn't say anything. Mazzum nodded in satisfaction. The human was learning who his real master was. Mazzum looked at Hannah for a moment before he said anything.

"Hold your hands out," Mazzum demanded harshly. "You will not fight your bonds. I do not like to see your skin damaged. If you fight again, I will knock you out."

Hannah sat still as Mazzum wrapped each of her wrists tightly with a length of fabric before he tied her wrists together behind her. Hannah sat still while he tied the remaining length to his own wrist. He then moved over to a tree across from them. Without another word, he closed his eyes.

Hannah stared up at the stars peeking through the canopy of trees above them. Throughout the night she listened to the soft snores of Bachman, who finally fell asleep in the early morning hours. Several times she would look to where Mazzum was leaning against the tree across from them only to discover him looking at her. She would turn her gaze back up to the glimmer of sky.

She couldn't understand why Mazzum wasn't concerned with her talking to Borj until she overheard a comment by Bachman to one of Mazzum's questions. Mazzum didn't think she could talk to him since she was a human. Bachman told him humans couldn't communicate telepathically. Mazzum spent every moment since they started out again asking questions about humans.

He wanted to know how males protected the females, how many young they could have, what Earth was like, what ways could a human female take a male and how often before she became too damaged to accept any more.

The questions were bad enough, but Bachman's answers to some of them were so horrible that it took everything in Hannah to not turn and confront him. When he described the things he did to other women, Hannah couldn't help but be happy he had a taste of his own medicine. He was one sick son-of-a-bitch.

They didn't stop again until a few hours ago and that was because it was too dark to continue. Hannah was thankful for Amurr's threat. He was larger and appeared to be the leader of the two brothers.

He also seemed meaner, Hannah thought in despair.

Hannah knew she was running out of time. So far, her gut wasn't telling her to do anything. She hoped her internal alarm would start giving her some type of signal soon because from the heated looks she was getting from Mazzum she wasn't sure how much longer she could depend on Amurr's threat to keep him away from her.

"Sleep, female. Tomorrow will be an even longer day and you will need your strength. As soon as Amurr is here, I plan to have you... many times," Mazzum said quietly with a twist to his lips.

"Why are you doing this?" Hannah asked in a frozen voice. "What makes a man like you?"

Mazzum just grinned darkly. "Sleep, female. If you survive, I might tell you," Mazzum said as he closed his eyes again.

Hannah knew she would get nothing else out of him. Closing her eyes, she sought out Borj needing his warmth to help her get through the night. She let her mind open and she pictured the pink sands he talked about wishing she could see it, feel it, and let it run through her fingers.

"Soon, my Hannah. Soon I will take you there and you will not only feel it as it runs through your fingers but I will love you among the silky grains. It is so soft you can sink down into it and sleep as if upon the clouds that drift across the sky," Borj said tenderly as he imagined wrapping his arms tightly around Hannah.

"Tomorrow I am going to try to escape. We are moving uphill. I still can't see anything but trees, but I can feel the change in the ground. It is getting

rockier. I think I can hear water in the distance as well," Hannah sent an image of where they were to Borj.

"J'kar and I are following the ravine near the river. We will be coming upon a set of smaller waterfalls soon. We are continuing through the night. I can feel you are closer," Borj assured her.

"Amurr will be meeting up with us in the afternoon. I'm afraid of what will happen when he gets here, Borj," Hannah said sadly.

Hannah felt a wave of warmth surround her before what Borj was saying registered. "Amurr will not be meeting you, Hannah. He has been caught. Do not let Mazzum know. He may decide to change his plans. I do not want to take a chance of him killing you and disappearing."

Hannah forced herself to remain relaxed. "Thank you. I love you so much, Borj. I want to spend the rest of my life showing you," Hannah said softly.

"I love you too, ku lei. Rest if you can. I will be with you soon," Borj said tenderly.

Hannah let her mind relax. She drifted off to dreams of pink sand, wild waves, and even wilder love making with Borj. As the night slowly faded to light, Hannah woke with a renewed determination to survive.

CHAPTER EIGHTEEN

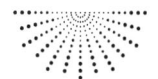

Borj stood on the lower end of a series of small waterfalls. Further up ahead, he could see a larger fall. A deep ravine ran down where the river cut through the rock over time. Borj pushed his fatigue aside. Merrick, Core, Te'mar and his father were in position at different sites throughout the area where different falls were located. Borj was so deeply imbedded in Hannah's mind he was seeing what she was seeing now. He refused to let her push him away or cut him off for any reason.

"J'kar," Borj called out in a low voice. "Hold up."

J'kar paused as he worked his way over a set of boulders. He turned waiting quietly as Borj stood still frowning. He was getting images from Hannah she probably wasn't even aware she was sending him. He saw the taller fall up ahead of them. They were climbing up a steep path leading up to the falls. He could almost feel the spray from the water as it fell around Hannah. The rocks were slippery. Hannah was in front. Borj watched as she turned. Bachman was behind her with Mazzum following up behind them.

Borj watched as if in slow motion as Hannah turned at a sound behind her. Bachman slipped on one of the stones. Mazzum moved to grip Bachman's arm, but suddenly he fell back a step with a stunned look on his face. Hannah's eyes widened as she saw the knife wound in Mazzum's side.

Bachman picked up one of the rocks lying loose and struck Mazzum on the side of the head, knocking him down and over the ledge of the narrow path. Borj lost sight of Bachman as Hannah's eyes followed the falling body of Mazzum as it disappeared before whipping back to Bachman so fast Borj felt a moment of disorientation.

"What is it?" J'kar asked in concern sliding back down the rock to grab hold of Borj when he put a hand to his head to steady himself.

"Bachman just attacked Mazzum. He stabbed him and knocked him over the edge of the path. They are at the upper falls," Borj said hoarsely as he saw Bachman was looking savagely at Hannah who was backing away from him. "He is going after Hannah," Borj said in a panic.

"Let's go," J'kar said, gripping Borj's arm and dragging him after him.

Both men started moving quickly over the boulders, cursing as they had to find different ways around them at times. Borj could feel Hannah's panic as she scrambled to get away from Bachman. J'kar was talking quickly into his comlink letting the others know they knew where Hannah was and they needed help.

Borj's heart was in his throat as he saw Hannah made it up to an upper ledge. She was trying to climb up a section of rock when Bachman came up behind her and grabbed her, throwing her down onto the slippery ledge. Borj felt murderous rage build inside him as he saw the look in Bachman's eyes as he stared down into Hannah's. The bastard was going to die a long and painful death if Borj had his way.

∽

Hannah watched as if in slow motion as Bachman stabbed Mazzum. Her instincts were screaming for her to get to the upper ledge of the falls. She didn't know why, but her gut was saying if she could get there she could get away. Hannah had been so focused on the feeling telling her to get to the top that she was almost oblivious to the two men behind her. She was moving with the easy grace of years of covering treacherous terrain.

When she heard Mazzum cursing as Bachman fell again, she thought this might be the break she needed. She was about to take off when something told her to look around. She never expected Bachman to have the nerve to attack Mazzum much less be successful at it. It was the look in Bachman's eyes, though, that made her frozen limbs defrost. He had murder and revenge in his eyes.

Hannah turned as quickly as she safely could and began climbing. She had to get to the ledge up above. She knew if she did, she had a chance to escape. Hannah felt a sense of triumph which quickly changed to horror as she realized the ledge lead to a steep climb straight up.

She was about five feet up when Bachman grabbed her leg pulling her off the rocks she was trying to climb. Hannah hit the slippery ledge hard on her hip, crying out at the impact. She quickly scrambled up to stand along the edge.

Bachman's grin was pure insanity. "Now that the bastard is dead, it is just you and me, darling. I want to know how to get off this fucking planet and you are going to tell me," Bachman said menacingly. "I hope you don't tell me too quickly, though. I'm looking forward to ringing every... little... piece... of... information... from... your... delicate... little... body," Bachman said slowly as he took a small, menacing step towards her.

Hannah glanced over her shoulder at the nearly forty foot drop to the basin far below where the waterfall fell into a pool of water before rushing down a series of smaller drops. Hannah looked back at Bachman with a small smile. Her gut was right. This was where she needed to be.

Looking at Bachman, Hannah tilted her head slightly to the side, staring him straight in the eye. "You'll never get off this planet alive," Hannah said softly. "I'm glad Mazzum showed you what it is like to be helpless. At least you had a taste of your own medicine before you die. My one hope is you can experience what you did to my sister when you stabbed her. Only, I don't think anyone is going to give a damn about you bleeding to death. Go to hell, Bachman. It's where you belong," Hannah added fiercely before she turned on her heel and jumped off the ledge.

Hannah felt a sense of freedom as her body fell through the air. She quickly tucked her arms to her side, drew in a deep breath, and braced for impact with the water below. As soon as her feet hit the water, she spread them to stop her momentum. She felt the current grab her immediately and suck her down to the next set of small falls. She didn't fight the current but let it take her body.

She briefly broke the surface and drew in a desperate breath of air before she was pulled back under. She felt her body hit a set of smaller boulders but she was able to push off of them before she felt herself falling again. She hit the bottom and tumbled along it, the force of it pushing precious breaths of oxygen out of her lungs.

Hannah pushed up with all her strength trying to slow her speed, but the current was too strong. She forced herself not to panic when her body started screaming for air. On one of her tumbles, she was able to pull in another desperate breath. Hannah felt her body free-falling again before she hit another turbulent wall of water.

She fought to get oriented enough to know which way it was to the shoulder of the river. She struggled trying to stop her tumbling body. She felt the current rip one of her shoes off as it pulled her relentlessly downstream.

Hannah's fingers grabbed one of the rocks when she was pushed up against it. She pulled her head above the water gasping. She grappled to get a better hold, but between the current and the slickness of the rock, she could feel her grip loosening.

"*Borj, I love you,*" Hannah called out as a sense of peace started to settle over her as a combination of cold and fatigue sapped what little energy she had left. "*I'm so sorry,*" Hannah whispered as her fingers lost their hold on the boulder and she slipped under the water one last time.

∼

Borj and J'kar were almost to the bottom of the first set of lower falls from the ledge where Hannah, Bachman, and Mazzum were when something told him to look up. His heart was in his throat as he saw Hannah standing on the edge of the ledge with Bachman moving menacingly towards her with a bloody knife in his hand. His heart actually stopped for a moment when he saw Hannah jump from the ledge into the falls. He watched in stunned disbelief as her delicate body hit the water below and disappeared only to resurface briefly as it was carried down one of the lesser falls.

"Go to her!" J'kar yelled out as he began moving rapidly towards Bachman. "I will get that bastard."

Borj turned and began moving rapidly down the edge of the ravine they were following. He practically flew over the boulders, jumping from one to another as he fought to keep his eyes on Hannah's body as it was being tossed about in the freezing, turbulent waters. He watched in horror as she slipped over another set of small drop-offs. He quickly rushed down the edge of the embankment, jumping onto one of the boulders over the water and slid into the water not far behind her.

He felt his own body lose weight as he fell through the air. He surfaced fighting to see where Hannah was. He caught a brief glimpse before she disappeared again under the water. He fought to push himself faster through the water after her. Up ahead, he caught a brief glimpse of her clinging to a boulder. Borj fought his way towards her. He was almost there when he felt her soft words echo through his mind before she slipped away from him.

Anguish unlike anything he knew filled Borj. With a cry of denial, he fought against the current trying to keep him from Hannah. Borj kicked out frantically with a burst of energy driven by fear and adrenaline.

He saw Hannah's body roll limply in the freezing water. Reaching out, his fingers twisted in the material of her shirt. He felt it slip from her body as the ruined material came undone from the knot she had tied. He reached out again with his other hand wrapping it around her cold arm. Pulling forcefully, he dragged Hannah's battered body to his, wrapping his arm more securely around her slender waist.

Borj pushed exhaustively against the current until he was in calmer water. Once he was able to get his feet under him, he stood on shaky limbs and pushed desperately towards shore. Borj collapsed down onto the small pebbles lining the riverbank. He turned Hannah's limp body over swearing when he saw her blue lips and sightless eyes.

He felt frantically at her neck. He couldn't find a pulse. He closed his eyes searching inward. He finally found what he was looking for. Wrapping the tiny sliver of light tightly with his own, he forced Hannah's life force to stay inside her. He refused to let her go. If she went, then they would go together.

"*Let me go,*" the faintest of whispers brushed his mind.

"*Never!*" Borj said gently as he began pushing the water out of Hannah's lungs and breathing for her. "*If you go, then I go with you. I told you we are one. I will always be there for you, Hannah, in life and in death.*"

"*Tired,*" Hannah whispered back as the tiny life force inside her flickered and dimmed.

"*Then, rest. I will take care of you,*" Borj said tenderly. "*Sleep as long as you need, but live… for us, for our children, for your family.*"

Borj felt the moment Hannah took her first breath on her own. Her eyes slowly closed and her color slowly changed from the pale blue to a soft, translucent pale peach. Borj sank down onto the rough pebbles and pulled Hannah's cold body into his arms.

Pulling his damp vest off, he gently covered her. His eyes followed the telling bruises covering her breasts, arms, and waist. He gently touched the cut along her throat with a shaky hand. Rocking back and forth, he lowered his head until it rested against Hannah's damp hair and cried silent tears. That was how his father found him a short time later.

Teriff walked slowly towards his younger son. Teriff felt his heart breaking at the sight of his proud son sitting holding his bond mate's fragile body against him protectively. He thought of Tresa and knew he would never survive the loss of her. He remembered his first meeting with Tink and how angry he was that such a tiny thing could be considered strong enough to be a mate to his son.

Now, he realized that despite their size, these human females possessed an unusual amount of strength and courage. J'kar called for them to come as soon as they saw Hannah jump. Merrick and Core retrieved Mazzum. He was wounded, but not dead… not yet anyway. J'kar told him of what happened. His son's mate was a true warrior.

"Te'mar is bringing a glider. We will have her to a healer soon," Teriff said gently as he laid his hand on Borj's shoulder.

"She does not deserve this," Borj said. "I should never have claimed her. I have done nothing but placed her in danger since she met me," Borj choked out.

"Nonsense," Teriff said gruffly. "She is a fighter. She is truly fit to be the mate of a Prime male."

"They hurt her," Borj said quietly. "She shielded me, but I see the evidence. They hurt her badly. She…" Borj looked at his father with such pain, Teriff fell back a step. "She protected me from it."

Teriff looked down at the pale face of his son's bond mate. She was breathing on her own, but not without difficulty. "Then you must protect her. Accept her and help her heal for it is your strength that will help her the most."

Borj watched as a group of warriors pulled Bachman and Mazzum down towards a ground transport that was about to land. "I demand the Right of Justice against all three men," Borj said emotionlessly, looking at two of the men being loaded onto the transport.

"Granted. I will stand as your second," Teriff said coldly watching as the transport lifted off.

CHAPTER NINETEEN

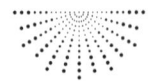

Hannah stirred enjoying the cool breeze floating in through the windows. She frowned as she looked around. It took a moment for her eyes to focus as she realized she was back in Borj's and her living quarters at the palace. Hannah sat up gingerly trying to figure out how she got here. The last thing she really remembered was slipping from the rock. Everything else was more like a dream.

"Not a dream, *ku lei*," Borj said softly, coming into the room.

Hannah's breath caught at how beautiful he looked. He was wearing nothing but a pair of low cut pants that were not fastened at the top. His hair was a little longer than she remembered as well. Hannah's eyes widened when she saw a long cut that was almost healed running across his chest. There was another one on his left arm.

"What happened to you?" Hannah asked anxiously reaching out a hand to touch it.

Borj sat down on the bed. His eyes closed briefly as he felt Hannah's hand gently trace the wounds he recently received. He opened his eyes to stare into the intense green ones of Hannah which were searching his with worry. A small smile curved his lips. She was safe. That thought sent waves of warmth and happiness through him. She was safe.

"It is nothing. I am almost healed," Borj said quietly letting his fingers run through the soft waves of Hannah's long hair.

Hannah fell back suddenly exhausted. She frowned up at Borj. "Why am I so tired?" she grumbled out. "I'm never this weak!"

Borj chuckled as he moved to lie down on top of the covers next to her. Pulling Hannah into his arms, he held her tightly against him enjoying her sweet scent and soft curves. They were both quiet for a moment before Borj spoke softly into Hannah's mind.

"*I almost lost you,*" Borj said quietly. "*When I was able to finally get to you, you were gone.*"

Hannah felt the shiver that ran through Borj's tall frame. "*How did you bring me back?*" Hannah asked tentatively.

"*I wrapped my life force around yours refusing to let the last tiny spark fade away. I was able to clear your lungs and you finally began breathing again on your own, but you were hurt from the many times you were thrown into the rocks along the river. Te'mar landed shortly after with a glider and I was able to transport you back to the village. It was closer than the palace. The healer was able to stabilize you, but you were still in danger. It took two days of healing before it was safe to transport you back to the palace. Once here, the healers continued to heal you,*" Borj explained in a husky voice.

"What about Bachman and the other two men," Hannah asked.

Borj let his one hand trace the long, healing scar on his chest. He felt Hannah's hand move to lay on top of his. He brushed a kiss across the top of her head and squeezed her gently before letting his fingers thread through hers.

"*They are dead. All three of them are dead,*" Borj told Hannah.

The breath Hannah was holding escaped in a soft exhale. "*How? What happened?*"

"*I invoked the Right of Justice. All three men committed a grievous injustice against what is mine,*" Borj said coldly.

Hannah rose up to look down into Borj's flaming silver eyes. "What is the Right of Justice? What are you not telling me?" Hannah asked, pulling her fingers from Borj's to trace the scar along his left arm.

Borj looked up into Hannah's soft eyes. "*Each man is given a chance to fight back. They choose one weapon. It was my right to give out justice. I fought each man. Each one died a very long, slow death for what they did to you, Hannah,"* Borj said as he cupped her cheek and leaned up to press a soft kiss to her lips.

"You could have been killed," Hannah murmured fearfully.

Borj's soft chuckle caressed Hannah's lips. *"No. I may be an Ambassador for our planet, but I am a warrior first. I was the stronger, more experienced warrior of the three. They stood little chance of defeating me. Besides, I had something to live for… you,"* Borj whispered as he brushed his lips back and forth across Hannah's.

"How long have I been sleeping?" Hannah asked puzzled. It seemed like a lot had happened in just a few short days.

"Oh, you've been sleeping for almost a week and a half, sweetheart," Tilly Bell said as she breezed into the bedroom carrying a tray, Angus right behind her.

Hannah squealed and ducked back under the covers. She wasn't wearing any clothes and the last thing she wanted was for her parents to see her in the buff. Hannah weakly punched Borj's arm when he sat up chuckling.

"This is not funny," Hannah hissed out glaring up at him from where she had the covers pulled up to her nose. "Didn't you lock the door?"

"Of course he did, love," RITA's voice said cheerfully. "Your mom overrode the command with a little help from me."

"Great, just great! Now we can't even have a locked door to keep them out," Hannah groaned out loud.

"Oh Angus! She really is alright," Tilly sniffed as she set the tray down next to the bed.

Hannah looked at the tears glittering in her mom's eyes and sighed. Her mom hardly ever cried except in cheesy romantic movies. Hannah saw the same look of anguish in her mom's eyes that was in them when she first saw her standing on the dock as Jacq brought her back when she was fifteen. Hannah sat up, tucking the sheet around her, and reached for her mom. Borj scooted over as Tilly Bell fell into her oldest daughter's arms sobbing.

Borj looked at Angus, who had tears in his own eyes. "I'm glad you're safe, Hannah bug."

Hannah looked up at her dad and gave him a watery smile. "Me, too. I love you both so much."

Tilly leaned back, smoothing her small hands over Hannah's damp cheeks. "How are you feeling?" Tilly asked softly.

Hannah knew her mom was asking her more than about her physical health. She was worried about Hannah's mental health. Both of them sat there for a moment, each reflecting on a different time and place. Hannah looked at her mom then at her dad and grinned.

"I'm doing good… really good," Hannah said, reaching a hand out to hold Borj's. "I'm going to be alright. I promise."

Tilly must have felt the truth in Hannah's words because she turned and sent a breathtaking smile to Angus. "She is going to be fine," Tilly whispered up to her husband.

Angus chuckled. Leaning over, he pulled his tiny wife up off the bed and into his arms. "Then, I suggest we give them some peace. I can think of a few things we can do on the way back to our living quarters. Are you interested?" Angus growled playfully.

Tilly's light laughter filled the air as she brushed her hand across Angus' chest. "What do you have in mind?" she whispered huskily.

"Will you two go get your own room?!" Hannah groaned out loudly. "This is way more information than I need to see this soon."

Angus chuckled as he swung his wife around to the door. Tilly turned just before he could scoot her through. "Oh! Before I forget, Hannah, we are having a movie marathon tonight! I had RITA download 'When Harry Met Sally', then we are doing a chick-flick night of romance! I can't wait. Lan and Brock have it set up on a big screen outside in the garden," Tilly said gleefully before Angus finished getting her out of the room.

Hannah dropped back down onto the bed with a chuckle. "You have no idea what you have done to your planet! A chick-flick movie night! The next thing will be the Tilly and Angus Bell Center for Sexual Discovery," Hannah joked looking up at the ceiling.

"What a wonderful idea!" RITA said. "I'll have to suggest that to your mom!"

Hannah jerked up. "RITA, don't you dare. It was a joke. RITA?

RITA!" Hannah called frantically trying to scramble out from under the covers only to fall back exhausted against them.

Borj laughed as he saw Hannah's flushed face. "My planet will be fine. Come, let me help you up. You will need to take things slowly until you recover completely," Borj said, lifting Hannah into his arms and walking with her to the cleansing room.

Hannah let her head drop back against Borj's shoulder. "Borj, do you think you can take me to that place you told me about? The one with the pink sand and water dragons," Hannah asked softly.

Borj's arms tightened around Hannah for a moment at her tentative question. "We will leave tomorrow and can stay as long as you like," he said huskily.

"I would like that," Hannah whispered sleepily.

Borj's lips curved in a tender smile as he brushed a kiss against Hannah's hair. He would bathe her and let her rest some more. Once she was asleep, he would make the necessary arrangements to be gone for an indefinite period of time. He would give Hannah all the time she needed to recover.

CHAPTER TWENTY

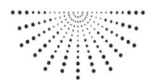

Hannah laughed as she adjusted the lens of her camera and snapped several more shots of the sea dragons playing in the surf. They were amazing creatures and she never got tired of watching them. Her head turned when she heard Borj call out to her and she waved her hand to let him know she heard him.

Turning, she slid off the rock she was lying on and felt the soft, pink sand slide between her bare toes. They had been at Borj's home on the ocean for almost a month and she still wasn't ready to return to the palace. It was amazing that it really wasn't that far from the palace.

Her mom and dad had visited with J'kar and Tink, who was beginning to show. She loved spending time with her family, but she enjoyed having Borj all to herself more. Maybe it was selfish of her, but she didn't care.

They had been here for a week before she was finally feeling like she had regained her strength. During that time, Borj treated her like she was made of spun glass. It was only when she tied him to the bed late one night and had her wicked way with him that she got the full reason out of him.

He thought she had been raped by Mazzum. He didn't want to say anything to her, but it finally came out during her interrogation session. She learned that little move from Tink, who told her how she did it to J'kar. The running of her tongue up and down his extended canines really did work! Once she did that then worked her way down his body, he sang like a canary telling her everything she wanted to know.

It took several hours of 'intensive interrogation' to finally convince him nothing happened. Yes, she had been scared. Yes, Mazzum was an ass to her. But, he was now a very dead ass thanks to her protective warrior who promised to come for her and did.

The weeks after that were filled with laughter and love. They played in the water, ate lunch and dinner often times watching the sea dragons playing in the surf, walked through the thick forest surrounding Borj's beautiful home, and made love... lots and lots of love.

Hannah smiled as she walked up to Borj. There was a handsome older man standing next to him. Hannah recognized the man as the healer from the palace. Smiling, she walked up to the men as they waited for her.

"Good morning, Saury. How are you doing?" Hannah asked with an inquiring smile.

Saury bowed slightly to Hannah before smiling in return. "I am most well, Lady Hannah. How are you feeling?"

"Never better," Hannah turned with a puzzled look at Borj. "Is something the matter?"

Borj flushed and looked at Saury quickly before he turned to Hannah and gripped her hand tightly. "I asked Saury to come and make sure you are well."

Hannah stared intently at Borj for a moment before shrugging her shoulder. "But, I told you yesterday that I was fine. I was a little queasy, but it passed as soon as I ate some toast."

Saury stepped forward. "His lordship is concerned that you might be with child. He wished for me to check."

Hannah stumbled back a little. She couldn't go far as Borj tightened his grip on her hand. Hannah's eyes flew from one man who was smiling gently to the other who was looking decidedly worried and...

hopeful? Hannah let her hand move down to her flat stomach. They had been making love like two rabbits in a marathon and they never used any type of contraceptive. Not to mention, Borj took every opportunity he could to bite her. Just the thought of it was enough to cause her to grow damp with desire. Hannah looked back up at Borj when she felt him squeeze her hand.

Blushing as she saw the knowing smile curve his lips as he sniffed the air, she scowled back at him. "Knock it off," she hissed under her breath.

"It won't take but a moment," Saury said gently.

Hannah looked at Borj again, then nodded almost reluctantly to Saury. She moved towards the house slowly. She listened as Saury told Borj about some of the things happening at the palace. The movie night must have been a success because there was one at least once a week. There had been demands for more, but Teriff had to limit it as the warriors were more interested in the movies than in training. Not to mention, they were beginning to demand a chance to find their bond mates.

A decision was made to let two warriors at a time go to Earth. RITA was giving out different coordinates so they were spread out. The warriors each had two weeks to find a bond mate. If they did not find one within that time, they had to return, but would be given another chance at a later date.

Tilly and Angus were giving the men tips and suggestions on how not to be detected and RITA was creating fake ID's and documents for all of them. Hannah just hoped Tansy never discovered what was going on! Mak was staying a little longer. Hannah hadn't heard the details but her gut was telling her something was going on.

Hannah smiled as she washed the light, flaky sand from her feet outside the door leading into an open living area. She set her cameras down on a table and turned to look at Saury. He looked around before motioning to the couch.

"If you could lie down and lift your top enough for me to scan you that would help," Saury said as he pulled a small scanning device out of the case he was carrying.

Hannah laid down on the couch. Borj moved quickly to scoot in at the top so she was resting her head in his lap. Hannah pulled her shirt up enough to expose her lower belly. Both she and Borj watched as Saury leaned over and ran the scanner first over her stomach, then over the rest of her. He looked at the readings with a small frown before running the scanner over her stomach several more times. When he was done, he took a few steps back looking at the readings again.

"What is it?" Borj asked anxiously.

Hannah reached up and gripped Borj's hand, curling her fingers around his.

Saury smiled at both of them reassuringly. "Hannah is fine. All of the readings are within the normal level for a human female according to the information RITA has given us," Saury said looking at the readings again. "Are multiple births common among humans?" Saury asked curiously.

Hannah paled at his question. "What do you mean 'multiple births'?" Hannah choked out.

"I am getting a double reading. It was the same as that of your sister from what I have seen of her report," Saury said with a puzzled frown.

"No, multiple births are not really all that common. Twins have never run in my family that I know of," Hannah whispered out as her other hand went to cover her stomach.

"It is the potent son-of-a-bitch problem your sister told us about," Borj said as a huge grin spread across his face. "I am a potent son-of-a-bitch, too!" Borj laughed.

Hannah's eyes flew to Borj's as she stared at him in shock. "I'll say! Oh. My. God. We're going to have babies," Hannah said softly. "My mom is going to have a cow."

Borj's eyes jerked down. "Why would your mother have a cow? How is that possible?"

Hannah chuckled. "It is an expression meaning she is going to be very excited."

Saury cleared his throat. "Would you care to know what you are having? You are actually several weeks along."

Hannah and Borj's eyes flew back to Saury. "You can tell? Already?" Hannah asked.

"Of course," Saury responded with amusement.

Borj was already nodding his head. "Yes. I want to know."

Saury glanced down at the readings on his scanner. "From the looks of it, you will be having one boy and one girl child. My congratulations to you both. Your father has requested I let him know as soon as possible. He wishes to announce it to everyone," Saury said with a chuckle.

Borj just nodded in a daze. Hannah looked back up at Borj whose face had paled considerably. She sat up, quickly turning to look at him in concern.

"What's wrong?" Hannah asked, touching his cheek.

Borj turned to look at Hannah with a sudden fierce expression on his face. "I will need to train. I will kill any male who even looks at my daughter. I will tear them apart with my bare hands. I will…," Borj was biting out.

Hannah pressed her lips to Borj's while waving Saury away with one hand. "You'll protect her and love her and support her in all her decisions," Hannah said softly before deepening the kiss.

Neither one of them heard Saury leave. "Come," Hannah said softly. "Come make love to me."

Hannah gently touched the face of the warrior who not only protected her, but loved her and made her finally feel safe. It didn't matter what happened in the past or even in the future as long as they were together. With him, she knew he would always be there for her and never let her go.

Borj stood up and swung Hannah into his arms. He felt the world shift beneath his feet settling into a calm, peaceful haven. From the first time he saw her image, he knew she was his life. Now, as he carried her towards their sleeping area, he knew he had been blessed by the Gods and Goddesses with a creature so beautiful, so strong, and so fierce she could only be a warrior created just for him.

To be continued… **Tansy's Titan**

Tansy Bell has a hidden talent that she uses to bring criminals to justice. She only goes after the worst of the worst, and this time might be her last.

Mak's oldest brother has found his bond mate among a newly discovered species called humans. They are surprisingly small and delicate, and Mak was always the wildest, most dangerous of his brothers, but the moment he sees an image of Tink's sister Tansy, he is captivated. Mak's long search for a bond mate is over. All he has to do now is find her location and convince her she belongs to him. If all else fails, he will just take her. After all, it is rare that even a Prime male can match his ferocity, and she is such a little thing.

It doesn't take Mak long to discover that a huge amount of trouble can come in a small package, and there is one female in the universe with the strength and determination of twenty Prime warriors who is not afraid to stand up to him – even if she is afraid to love him.

Check out the full book here: books2read.com/TansysTitan

Or read on for a sneak peek into a new series!

Hunter's Claim
The Alliance Book 1

USA Today Bestseller!
The Alliance came in peace, but Earth was thrown into chaos....

Alone in a world gone mad with just her teenage sisters, Jesse Sampson has seen the savage side of human nature and found they are not much different from the aliens who conquered Earth, but she's kept what's left of her family alive, that's all that matters—until Jesse sees an alien who will suffer a horrible death if she does not free him from his human captors. Her own nature won't allow her leave him to his fate, and that decision changes everything.

Check out the full book here: books2read.com/Hunters-Claim

ADDITIONAL BOOKS

If you loved this story by me (S.E. Smith) please leave a review! You can discover additional books at: http://sesmithfl.com and http://sesmithya.com or find your favorite way to keep in touch here: https://sesmithfl.com/contact-me/ Be sure to sign up for my newsletter to hear about new releases!

Recommended Reading Order Lists:
http://sesmithfl.com/reading-list-by-events/
http://sesmithfl.com/reading-list-by-series/

The Series

Science Fiction / Romance

Dragon Lords of Valdier Series
It all started with a king who crashed on Earth, desperately hurt. He inadvertently discovered a species that would save his own.

Curizan Warrior Series
The Curizans have a secret, kept even from their closest allies, but even they

are not immune to the draw of a little known species from an isolated planet called Earth.

Marastin Dow Warriors Series
The Marastin Dow are reviled and feared for their ruthlessness, but not all want to live a life of murder. Some wait for just the right time to escape....

Sarafin Warriors Series
A hilariously ridiculous human family who happen to be quite formidable... and a secret hidden on Earth. The origin of the Sarafin species is more than it seems. Those cat-shifting aliens won't know what hit them!

Dragonlings of Valdier Novellas
The Valdier, Sarafin, and Curizan Lords had children who just cannot stop getting into trouble! There is nothing as cute or funny as magical, shapeshifting kids, and nothing as heartwarming as family.

Cosmos' Gateway Series
Cosmos created a portal between his lab and the warriors of Prime. Discover new worlds, new species, and outrageous adventures as secrets are unravelled and bridges are crossed.

The Alliance Series
When Earth received its first visitors from space, the planet was thrown into a panicked chaos. The Trivators came to bring Earth into the Alliance of Star Systems, but now they must take control to prevent the humans from destroying themselves. No one was prepared for how the humans will affect the Trivators, though, starting with a family of three sisters....

Lords of Kassis Series
It began with a random abduction and a stowaway, and yet, somehow, the Kassisans knew the humans were coming long before now. The fate of more than one world hangs in the balance, and time is not always linear....

Zion Warriors Series

Time travel, epic heroics, and love beyond measure. Sci-fi adventures with heart and soul, laughter, and awe-inspiring discovery...

Paranormal / Fantasy / Romance

Magic, New Mexico Series
Within New Mexico is a small town named Magic, an... unusual town, to say the least. With no beginning and no end, spanning genres, authors, and universes, hilarity and drama combine to keep you on the edge of your seat!

Spirit Pass Series
There is a physical connection between two times. Follow the stories of those who travel back and forth. These westerns are as wild as they come!

Second Chance Series
Stand-alone worlds featuring a woman who remembers her own death. Fiery and mysterious, these books will steal your heart.

More Than Human Series
Long ago there was a war on Earth between shifters and humans. Humans lost, and today they know they will become extinct if something is not done....

The Fairy Tale Series
A twist on your favorite fairy tales!

A Seven Kingdoms Tale
Long ago, a strange entity came to the Seven Kingdoms to conquer and feed on their life force. It found a host, and she battled it within her body for centuries while destruction and devastation surrounded her. Our story begins when the end is near, and a portal is opened....

Epic Science Fiction / Action Adventure

Project Gliese 581G Series
An international team leave Earth to investigate a mysterious object in our solar system that was clearly made by someone, someone who isn't from

Earth. Discover new worlds and conflicts in a sci-fi adventure sure to become your favorite!

New Adult / Young Adult

Breaking Free Series
A journey that will challenge everything she has ever believed about herself as danger reveals itself in sudden, heart-stopping moments.

The Dust Series
Fragments of a comet hit Earth, and Dust wakes to discover the world as he knew it is gone. It isn't the only thing that has changed, though, so has Dust…

ABOUT THE AUTHOR

S.E. Smith is an *internationally acclaimed, New York Times* **and USA TODAY Bestselling** author of science fiction, romance, fantasy, paranormal, and contemporary works for adults, young adults, and children. She enjoys writing a wide variety of genres that pull her readers into worlds that take them away.

Printed in Great Britain
by Amazon